Sylvia McNicoll

Walking A Thin Line

D0456412

cover art by

Colin Poole

Scholastic Canada Ltd.

onto, New York, London, Sydney, Auckland

For Mom

Scholastic Canada Ltd.
123 Newkirk Road, Richmond Hill, Ontario, Canada L4C 3G5
Scholastic Inc.
555 Broadway, New York, NY 10012, USA
Scholastic Australia Pty Limited
PO Box 579, Gosford, NSW 2250, Australia
Scholastic New Zealand Limited
Private Bag 94407, Greenmount, Auckland, New Zealand
Scholastic Publications Ltd.
Villiers House, Clarendon Avenue, Leamington Spa,
Warwickshire CV32 5PR, UK

Canadian Cataloguing in Publication Data

McNicoll, Sylvia, 1954 –

  Walking a thin line

ISBN 0-590-12379-3

I. Title.

PS8575.N52W34 1997   jC813'.54   C97-930054-1

PZ7.M36Wa 1997

5 4 3 2 1   Printed in Canada   7 8 9/9

Chapter 1

Is she fatter than I am? It's a game I often play. I look at a girl who's on the chunky side and ask myself that question. Right now I was winning. As Andrea Partington swish-swished up to the front of the room to deliver her presentation, she beat out everyone in grade seven in the weight category, including me. She's been the heavyweight champion ever since I can remember. Not immense, but always a little on the pudgy side. Only in the last year, I've become a contender too.

Andrea's dress hung straight down from her bust, making her body look like one solid block. A blue flowered block. And of course she wore pantyhose that made an awful sound. Swish-swish. Swish-swish. Finally the noise stopped as Andrea turned to face the class.

Her hands shook as she raised her cue cards. Not the best sign.

I shifted in my chair and felt the crack pinch the back of my thigh. I moved away from it, wincing at my best friend Stephanie. She sat next to me,

1

shaking her head. "Change the chair," she mouthed at me, dodging a look from Ms Smyrnios.

I shrugged, shifted again and drummed my fingers on the desk. *Come on, Andrea. Let's go.*

Her doll-blue eyes glanced at the cards and then looked wildly around the room. Finally they met mine and stopped there. You can do it, Andrea, you can do it.

She bit her lip and dropped one hand from the cards. I watched it clench and unclench. Then she cleared her throat and licked her lips. Her face got even pinker than usual and she tucked her dangly blond hair behind her ears. Then she grabbed hold of the cue cards with both hands again and started.

"When I grow up . . . um . . . When I grow up, I want to be a vet . . . veterinarian . . . uh . . . in an equine practice mostly because . . . "

At the back of the room, Matthew snorted. Carlos whinnied back softly.

With all her attention focussed on Andrea, Ms Smyrnios didn't seem to notice, or maybe she decided to ignore The Boys. But Andrea heard. Her eyes lifted and locked onto mine, sending me quiet panicky pleas. *Help me, Lauren. Help me.*

Keep going, I yelled inside my head. *Just ignore them and keep going. Don't let them see that it hurts.* I'd learned that from my sister Patricia back when I started school. Patricia, in grade six at the time, had attracted a gang of kids calling her names because she was the slowest in her class. My big strong sister who could have easily punched out the ringleader simply smiled at him and walked away, dragging me by the hand. Never let them see that it hurts, she had told me. They'll only tease you more.

But Andrea didn't have an older sister — or anyone else, really, besides me. She wasn't always the easiest person to get along with. I should have turned around and told Carlos and Matthew to shut up. I should have, but at that moment Andrea began again.

"I want to be a veterinarian. I'll work at the Triple–R Ranch this summer cleaning out the stables. Hopefully I'll get a scholarship to the University of Guelph . . . "

In mid-thought she forgot what came next and shuffled her cards frantically. One card dropped. She made a quick grab for it and the rest fluttered from her hands to the floor.

Would she pull it together? Sitting up front, I could have jumped up and gathered them for her, but instead I shut my eyes for a second and sighed.

Another soft whinny came from the back as Andrea bent over to retrieve the notes. "Aw gees," I grumbled to Stephanie as I slid out of my seat to help Andrea.

Too late. Andrea threw the cards down again and tore out of the room.

Nobody snickered now. I shrugged my shoulders and sighed again. Then I stooped down carefully, so that no one would laugh, and picked up the cards in no particular hurry.

Ms Smyrnios frowned, folding her arms in front of her. "That's too bad," she finally said, but she didn't run after Andrea like Ms Hick had in grade five when Andrea spilled coloured water all over her science project. Or like Mr. Philips did in grade six when Andrea forgot her only line, "Don't Waste Water," in our environmental play. Andrea could never handle doing anything in front of the class. But grade-seven teachers didn't chase after students — they needed to be tough like their kids.

I scanned Andrea's cue cards. In neat point form, her life plan looped across the cards. Stuff like:

— Take zoology, chemistry & physics in high school
— Two years pre-veterinarian studies
— Four years at Ontario Veterinary College
— Buy ranch and board horses; set up practice
— Save to buy a mare and a stallion
— Buy more horses as per income ($35,000-50,000 annual)

Okay, so she was a little obsessed. But her presentation could have been great. Andrea showed a clear direction for her life. She seemed in control — something no one expected from a round-cheeked, doll-eyed girl. She'd done way more research than I had too. Basically my Nanna

Dreyburgh just feeds me my lines straight from her talk shows. I stacked the cue cards on Ms Smyrnios's desk.

"We–ll," Ms Smyrnios said, drawing the word out. "We'll give Andrea some time to collect herself. Matthew, you seem to have a lot of energy this morning. Perhaps you would like to give your presentation next, since we're ahead of schedule now."

Matthew's mouth dropped and he shook his head.

"Carlos, how about you?"

"No, Ms Smyrnios. I left my notes at home." Carlos smirked at Matthew.

"Well then, who's next on my list? Jay Friessen. I'm sure you brought your cue cards today."

Jay pulled his long body up straight in the chair, sucked at his lip and flipped his pencil over a few times. He's adorable even when he's in trouble. Here was my chance to rescue him and maybe score some points.

"Ms Smyrnios," I half raised my hand as I interrupted, "I'm ready and I'd like to get my speech over with, if it's okay with you."

Ms Smyrnios stared Jay down for an extra moment. "Mr. Friessen?"

Jay shrugged and nodded.

"Very well, Lauren."

I smiled as I walked to the front. Then I stood there, digging my fists into my overall pockets and looking over the rows of faces. I focussed on

Stephanie. Hers had to be the skinniest face in the whole room. Her cheeks looked sucked in and her cheekbones stuck out. She gave me a thumbs-up sign and then rolled her eyes into her head so that only the whites showed. It's a special effect she's mastered for the horror videos we make and it always cracks me up, so I had to look away. But as I scanned the other faces, something else really bothered me.

With Andrea gone, my face was the fattest in the room.

I had to force myself to think about something else or I'd want to run away too. "You have a pretty face," Nanna Dreyburgh always tells me. "See the way your hair frames it almost in a perfect heart shape. Your skin is so fair and your hair so dark, you're like Snow White."

"Such a pretty face" is what people usually say about Andrea. They maybe don't say the end of the sentence, but what they really mean is "if only she could lose just a little weight."

I took a deep cleansing breath, in through the nose, out through the mouth, a relaxation technique my mother told me about when she returned from a sales conference. Now I glanced around the room, smiling.

All the rows of kids at my command, waiting for me to speak — I tried to make eye contact with each one of them for a quick moment. Two moments for

Jay Friessen, long-legged, dark and smiling in appreciation at the back. And when I saw his grey eyes laughing, I relaxed my hands, opening my fingers and wiggling them a bit. He thinks I'm funny, I realized. He likes me. Another breath and I started:

"I don't know what I want to be when I grow up. I mean, I've just turned thirteen and so far I haven't found anything I really love — like Jay with his computers, or Andrea and her horses." I stopped and looked at Ms Smyrnios for a moment. Her mouth pursed, her eyes said nothing. I needed to win her over.

"But my Nanna Dreyburgh says if you have no idea what you want to do for a living, you may as well pick the job that pays the most."

That line got a couple of snickers. Ms Smyrnios's lips stretched a little.

"So I found this article in *Chatelaine* on what work is worth. And the stuff in it really surprised me. For example, did you know a violinist for the Winnipeg Symphony Orchestra makes twenty-six thousand dollars a year? Well, that sounds like a lot more than what I make for allowance, but then I don't have to buy a ten-thousand-dollar violin or a five-thousand-dollar bow. And a taxi driver in Halifax makes nine hundred fifty dollars a month including tips, while a hot-dog vendor in Toronto can earn eighteen thousand dollars a year. Did you know an office-tower window cleaner makes an average of six hundred fifty dollars per month? That's in season."

Ms Smyrnios's mouth curved upwards a little now. Research is what she wanted. I didn't really have to decide what I wanted to be when I grew up as long as it looked like I'd done work to *not* decide.

"I also read that this guy, I forget what his name is now, makes from zero to seven thousand dollars a speech. So doing speeches in class could be good practice for a well-paying job."

Ms Smyrnios smiled and nodded now.

"Or maybe not. It depends on whether you were doing the talk for zero or for seven thousand dollars. What I ended up picking for my future job was telephone operator."

I stopped then and made eye contact with a few kids. Kim's eyes fluttered up at me from the *Ms Mode* magazine she was studying. It's what she wants to be when she grows up — a Mode model — and the magazine had been her prop. She tossed her thick red hair back, throwing up her chin as though an invisible camera was clicking somewhere. Next to her, Jay again, smooth and smiling, with his arms stretched back and folded behind his head. My eyes met his. His gangly legs, crossed at the ankles under the seat ahead of him, made him look totally relaxed. He yawned and whispered something to Matt and I wanted to force him to sit up and pay attention to me. I wanted to make him laugh; it was what I did best. But I needed an amazing punch line. Sucking in another cleansing breath, I took a step closer to the class and went for one.

"I thought I could do a better job than most telephone people. You know those voices that say 'Please hang up and try your call again.' I could put more expression in my voice, be more honest. I'd say 'Hey loser, you dialled the wrong number. Be more careful next time.' Or instead of saying 'The number you have dialled is no longer in service,' I'd say, 'They moved and didn't bother to tell you, sucker!'"

Jay grinned now and looked over to Matthew, who laughed. I checked out Ms Smyrnios. It could go either way with her at this point. One lip curled downward and her chin rested on her hand.

"Lauren," she said.

"Yes, Ms Smyrnios."

"You're off topic. Get on with it."

"Yes, Ms Smyrnios."

Jay winked at me. I suddenly felt like the most beautiful girl in the room. I started again: "But I chose the job because I made a mistake. I told Nanna Dreyburgh about being an operator and she told me she used to work as a manager for the phone company. They were the first people who hired and promoted women and she thought I'd

9

made a good choice. When I told her that operators made one hundred twenty-five dollars a half hour though, she wanted to see the *Chatelaine* article. That's when Nanna explained that a call girl wasn't the same thing as a telephone operator."

Now Jay bent over laughing. Did he like me, did he like me?

Ms Smyrnios frowned. We both knew I understood what a call girl did and how that shouldn't be mentioned in a classroom. I needed to regain some ground with her.

"Seriously though, I think the world is changing so fast — it's really hard when you're in grade seven to plan what you want to be. My mother studied to be a teacher but there were no jobs when she graduated, so she became a real estate agent. She loves it too. Maybe computers will operate all the phones when I graduate or maybe there won't be any phones at all. What I want to do is decide what things I like doing. I'll go to university when I finish high school and try all kinds of courses. In my summer vacations I'll work at different part-time jobs. I hope in that way to come to the right job for me. And if not, I'll change jobs and try again. I read that the average person changes careers three point five times in their life." I stopped and smiled in Ms Smyrnios's direction.

She smiled too. Another statistic that smelled of time spent in the library. It came from Nanna, of course, and therefore probably from Oprah. "Thank you for listening." I tipped my head slightly.

"Very good, Lauren. Now with next month's presentation, you'll want to think about the Halton Public Speaking Contest."

Next month, ha! It's something I'd been thinking about since grade one when I'd emceed the primary winter concert. All the applause, the birthday invitations that followed — for a while the kids even picked me first to be on their dodgeball teams. Imagine what it would be like in grade seven when I could finally enter the Halton Public Speaking Competition.

And now it was only three months away. I could hear the applause already.

But it was Ms Smyrnios clapping and the rest of the class joining in.

Only when the last hand stopped did I head back to my seat.

"Great!" Stephanie whispered at me.

I thought so. The class was pretty quiet now, filling out evaluation forms, giving me an A and giving Andrea who knows what. I sank into my chair with relief.

Crack! The small split in my chair opened and my body sagged down suddenly. Hoping no one had noticed, I quickly checked around me.

Stephanie shrugged one shoulder but there it was. Snicker, snicker. Matthew and Jay thought breaking a chair was pretty funny. I felt my face burn red hot and my eyes ache to cry. I shut them. Now I felt as heavy as the lady I'd seen in a photograph in *The Sun*, the one whose flesh hung in shapeless white waves over itself. She'd weighed over five hundred pounds when she died, and needed to be buried in a piano case because she couldn't fit into any coffin.

In through the nose, out through the mouth — I could get over this. Slowly, I raised myself and shifted my weight so that I wouldn't need to change chairs right that moment. The whole class didn't have to know. Jay and Matthew were still grinning when I glanced back. I couldn't think of a funny thing to say, but I pretended to laugh with them. *Never let them see that it hurts.* That's what Andrea needed to learn.

"Do you think I'm fat?" I asked Stephanie later at lunch. We were the first ones at the table and as usual we stacked our desserts in the centre, ready to trade.

Stephanie acted as though she hadn't heard me. "Hey, look at the ingredients for these butter tarts." She started reading from the package she pulled in front of her. "Sugar, cornstarch, flour, vegetable shortening and whole egg substitutes. There's no butter in these. Why don't they call them vegetable shortening tarts?"

"Stephanie, I asked you a question." I stared at her, not believing she couldn't toss off a quick no.

"Yeah, but I asked you one too. I mean why should they call them butter tarts if there isn't any butter? Isn't it like false advertising?" Stephanie busied herself undoing the wrapper.

"Stephanie," I repeated, "am I fat?"

Stephanie stopped fiddling and frowned. "Lauren, you're my best friend."

"Aw, right! That means I am. Thanks a lot Steph."

"You're not fat. You just have big bones. Are you eating that other vegetable shortening tart? Or are you swapping for my chocolate cupcake?"

"Have them both. I've lost my appetite."

"Great." Stephanie snatched the tart and wolfed it down. "You're not eating your sandwich either? Did your grandmother give you Patricia's liverwurst again?"

"No." I could smell Nanna's special egg salad, a faint hint of onion mixed with the sweet scent of mayonnaise. My stomach growled. My hand rested on the sandwich.

"Aw c'mon. You aren't fat!"

"I broke a chair today, Steph. Did you hear the guys? They were killing themselves over it."

"I told you to change that chair."

"Well, I had to wait till after class, didn't I?"

"I guess . . . Anyway, they were just hacking

around. You didn't mind when they laughed at your speech." Stephanie licked icing off her fingers. "It was really great. You're on your way, Lauren. I can see a big brass trophy in your future."

"Yeah, well, I still have to come up with a good topic." I unwrapped the sandwich and bit into one half, wondering, could Jay love a girl for her speaking ability? "Do you think he likes me?" I stared into the crowd of lunch-timers, seeing none of them, imagining only one grinning face with laughing grey eyes.

"Who, Jay?"

"Uh huh."

"Why don't we just ask him?" Stephanie stood up and looked around the room.

"Steph, no!"

She sat down again.

"Get someone else to ask him when I'm not around. Pass him a note or something," I said.

"Sounds good. Here's a paper." She whipped a lined sheet from her binder. "And here's a pen. What should I write?"

"How about 'Lauren Dreyburgh is cute: True or False. Please circle one.' "

"Gotcha." She finished the note off with a big smiley face. Then she waved at someone in the cafeteria line. "Kim, come eat with us!" she called.

Of course! Sitting so close to him, Kim could pass Jay the note.

Kim finished collecting her change from the cashier and turned to us, smiling. Tray in hand, she strode our way using her long-legged runway walk. She didn't notice Emily Urbaniak, behind her, imitating her made-for-the-runway stride.

"Could you give this to Jay for us?" Stephanie asked Kim as she sat down beside us.

"Yeah sure." She tucked the folded paper into her jean pocket. "Do you have the answer to question ten in math?"

"Right here." Stephanie flipped open her binder to the math divider.

"That's okay, I'll grab it after I eat." Kim picked up a lettuce leaf and nibbled at it as if she weren't really hungry at all, just posing for a salad ad. She seemed to be looking for something or somebody, an imaginary photographer or film crew standing somewhere behind me, and didn't pay much attention to any of us. Good thing she hadn't spotted Emily.

"Hey, Lauren," Stephanie said, "It's Cheap Tuesday at Super Video. Want to rent that 'Frankenbeast' game again after school?"

"Sure. I have some allowance left."

"Uh-oh, here comes Andrea," Kim warned. "You'd think somebody as smart as her would do something with that body. Lauren, duck, maybe she won't see you."

"I can't do that." I could hear Andrea's pantyhose swishing and turned to face the sound.

Andrea waved and I returned the motion. Eyes wide with relief, she rushed over, placed her tray on our table and slid onto a chair.

Kim stopped nibbling and raised her eyebrows into arrows as she stared openly at Andrea.

Andrea unfolded a napkin into her lap. "Would you pass me the salt, please?" she asked, huffing to catch her breath.

Without breaking her stare Kim slammed down the shaker in front of Andrea.

"Thank you."

"You're welcome," Kim answered, mimicking Andrea's good manners. She watched as Andrea shook a layer of salt onto her plate. "Andrea, don't you care about what you eat?" she asked.

"Huh?" Andrea stabbed her fork through a french fry.

Kim's face pulled together in disgust. "At least think of your poor horse, why don't you. How will it be able to carry you?"

Why does Kim say awful stuff like that? My mouth fell open and my brain tried to send words to my lips. But my brain failed. Kim stood up, snatched Stephanie's math answers and left.

Stephanie's brain worked a little better, but not much. "Do you still go riding every weekend, Andrea?" she asked, as though that had been the topic we were discussing.

Andrea nodded, keeping her head down. She

stabbed another fry and continued chewing slowly. Only when her plate was clean did she finally speak again. "Ms Smyrnios said I can still earn an A in Language Arts if I do my speech over in front of the class."

I shut my mouth and looked at Stephanie. If Andrea was going to ignore Kim's crack, I guess we could too. "You don't want to do that," I said, relieved at the change of subject. "What will you get without it?"

Andrea wiped her mouth with her napkin. "B," she said after a moment. "But I have to get an A, Lauren. I always get As. Can you help me after school?"

"Lauren's playing 'Frankenbeast' with me," Stephanie answered.

"Aw c'mon, please? You can play that any time."

I raised my eyebrows and shrugged my shoulders at Stephanie. "All right. Are you coming over then?" I asked.

Stephanie kicked me under the table.

"No, Mom's showing some houses today and I promised to mind the twins. But you can come to my house, Lauren."

"Oh great, Noah and Neil. How am I supposed to help you with the terrors around?"

"They'll be fine, really. I'll bribe them. Mom shouldn't be that long — "

"Oh no!" I'd stopped paying attention to what

Andrea was saying. Looking past Andrea's shoulder, I spotted Jay in the cafeteria line and Kim swinging over that way, her hand reaching into a pocket. "Don't give it to him *now!*" I begged softly.

I should have known. She smiled and looked toward our table.

Jay read the note she handed him, his brow furrowed. It seemed like a tough decision. He shrugged his shoulders. Then he leaned over and whispered something into Kim's ear. Kim brushed her fingers through her hair, fluffing it up. She blushed and laughed. Then she walked over to our table.

"About what you asked him," Kim said. "He says he likes you as a friend and that you're sort of cute." Now Kim lowered her voice. "But he thinks you could be a real knockout if you lost some weight." She glanced Andrea's way, then dismissed us both and swung off to sit at the guys' table.

In my mind I could feel that classroom chair split beneath me again. This time I imagined myself sinking to the floor with the whole cafeteria pointing at me and laughing, and at that moment I pushed away the rest of my sandwich and made up my mind never to eat again.

Chapter 2

By the end of the day my stomach sounded like a bowling alley. I knew I would need to eat something soon or die. Supper. I should at least hold out till supper.

"Nan, what's to eat?" I called the moment I stepped through the door. I heard the television blaring and followed the aroma of baking chocolate down the hall to the kitchen.

Bent over an open oven, her bottom stretched against polyester pants, Nanna pulled out a sheet of cookies. Her glasses steamed slightly so she lifted the purple frames to rest on top of her white hair. All her wrinkles smiled at me as she straightened. "Where's Stephanie?"

"Uh, Steph went straight home because I promised to help Andrea with her speech today."

"That's too bad. I made your favourite, reverse chocolate chip cookies."

"Oh no!"

I walked over to the stove where Nanna had laid the cookie sheet, and stared at them. The melting white chips oozed slightly and the outer layer of the cookies had split apart. I could see they were soft and chewy, just the way I loved them. The bowling ball in my stomach crashed into the pins.

Nanna hugged me. She felt soft and inviting like the cookies. "So how was your day?"

I pulled away. "Terrible, Nan."

"There, there." She touched my shoulder. "You know, the best thing about a bad day is that the next one has to be better." She gently guided me down the steps from the kitchen area to the family room. Mom was big into open concept when we bought the house, which makes it easier now for Nan to catch all her shows.

"Nan, I have to lose weight."

"Really? Let's just sit here on the couch and watch 'The Health Corner' while we wait for the cookies to cool. You can tell me all about it."

I'd hoped she'd tell me that I was perfect just the way I was, that I had such a pretty face, just like Snow White. Instead Nan's eyes trained themselves on the screen as we sat down.

"You know, when I was your age I was as skinny as a broomstick." Nanna held up a finger to show me the imaginary stick, but her purple frames still faced the screen.

What happened? I wanted to ask, but I didn't want to hurt her feelings. She didn't look bad for sixty-seven, just slightly pear-shaped. She always dressed in dark-coloured slacks with elasticized waistbands. They didn't make zippers like they used to, she claimed. Over the slacks she wore a long top that covered her butt and stomach. For her age she seemed perfect.

"Yup," she said, shifting her gaze away from the set for a quick second. "Skinny as a broomstick, till I had your father and then your uncles."

"Nan, I'm this big and I haven't had any kids. What am I going to look like when I'm your age?"

"Better. They'll have perfected facelifts by then." I knew Nan's attention was split between me and The Shopping Network. It seemed to be winning so I gave up and listened along.

A deep butterscotch voice crooned on about how difficult it was to eat enough vegetables every day. A lady's hand appeared on the screen, shaking some green capsules from a bottle onto a table. "Just three of these every day, and you never have to look at another broccoli floret in your life."

Now the whole lady appeared. She and Butterscotch Voice were sitting around the table with an assortment of small bottles standing next to the green capsules. Across the left corner of the screen the words Veggie Pills appeared. Across the right the time flashed, 3:00, meaning there were three minutes to call in and order. "You remember as kids how we used to have to eat all our green beans or our spinach and we couldn't step away from the table till we were all done? Well, you don't have to do that to your own children." Blah, blah, blah. 2:30 flashed at the bottom. What more could two people possibly find to say over the next two and a half minutes about these boring little vitamin pills.

Nan grinned. "Twenty-six fifty. Regularly priced at thirty-two seventy-five. Broccoli's ninety-nine cents a bunch over at the Price Chopper today."

Nan loved outsmarting The Shopping Network. She struggled to shift around on the couch. I noticed the copper anklets bulging through her knee-highs above her white sneakers.

"Those arthritis anklets don't seem to be working for you, Nan."

She winced. "There's a thirty-day money-back guarantee, don't you worry, Lauren. Besides, who knows how bad it might be without the anklets."

The butterscotch voice crooned on about vita-mins and nutrition. I noticed that he only needed to speak another thirteen seconds now. How could he find so much to say about these stupid little pills? How had he trained for this job? Maybe he'd tried out for the public speaking contest at school too. A salesperson for The Shopping Network, that seemed to be an even better future job than telephone operator. It might be fun to yack and yack about some strange item you were selling.

Different objects appeared on the screen now.

"Oh look, Nan, earrings to help your arthritis." The camera zoomed in on the same lady as she carefully screwed on penny-sized golden earrings.

Nan leaned forward, placing her hands over the little sewn-in creases of her slacks.

"And all you have to do is wear them?" the butterscotch voice asked.

"That's right. You put them on and your appetite will vanish. Say goodbye to painful dieting. It's just that simple."

"Run and get us some cookies," Nan suggested.

"Wait, I want to hear this."

"Here's a 'before' picture of a satisfied customer." It was the piano-case lady of my nightmare. "And here," the lady said, showing a picture of a slim woman holding out a pair of jeans from her stomach, with space to fit two more people, "is the same customer just ten months later, weighing one hundred and five pounds less."

"And all she did was wear the earrings? She did not attend any weight-loss clinics or participate in any special exercise programs?" Mr. Butterscotch asked, right on cue.

"That's correct."

I looked to the left-hand corner of the screen now. Regular price was $57.95, the Health Corner price was $39.99. The 3:00 flashed in the other corner.

Nan hoisted herself up and headed for the cookie sheet.

I looked at her large bottom. She used to be as skinny as a broomstick. . . .

A picture of Jay flashed in my brain, long-legged, long-armed, with smiling grey eyes that winked at me. I could be a knockout if I lost some weight, he'd said. I'm sort of cute and I'm funny, but I could be a knockout. Another picture flashed in my mind. It was me as the piano-case lady, folds of flesh hanging from me, with my bottom inflated to size hippopotamus. Suddenly there seemed to be only one answer. "Nan, Nan," I shouted. "I need those earrings."

Nan concentrated on slipping her spatula under the cookies and sliding them gently onto a plate. "I'll get us some milk," she answered.

"EZ-Slim earrings," said Butterscotch Voice. "I can imagine these will be quite the rage for all you ladies getting ready for those swimsuits." Blah, blah, blah. 2:00 flashed. Only two minutes left to buy them.

How much money did I have in the bank? Twenty-five dollars, plus five dollars in my potato bank, and with allowance . . . "Nan, I want to buy these, but I don't have a chequing account. Can you help me?"

Nan's body was totally hidden by the fridge door now. "What's that, Lauren?" She poured us each a glass of milk and brought over the cookies.

The one-minute sign flashed. "Nan, please. Help

me. I *have* to have those earrings." I searched the cradle for the cordless phone. Not there. I pressed the intercom button to track it down and pawed through a pile of magazines when its signal beeped.

"Got it." I gasped. I keyed in the 1-800 number. The ten-second signal flashed. Nine...eight...seven ...six...*Ring! Ring!* Five...four...three...Weren't they going to answer? Two...one...Finally! "Here Nan, take it. I'll pay you back, honest. Just give them your credit card number."

Nan looked puzzled but spoke normally to the order person. She motioned for me to get her purse and I rushed to the hall closet to find it. Nan was a life saver, I had to hand it to her. She took her wallet from the purse and flipped it open to read the credit card number.

Meanwhile I picked a warm cookie off the plate. I bit into it. Mmmm! When the earrings get here, I'll never look at another one of these.

Nan placed the phone on the cradle when she'd finished. "I hardly think you need to lose weight, Lauren. But you girls, you're always after the perfect figure," she said, picking up a cookie of her own. She winked and held out the plate. "Well, I don't suppose those earrings can do you any harm. And it doesn't hurt to cut down on the junk food."

"Nan, you're offering me a cookie."

"My cookies aren't junk food! They're homemade, with real butter and cocoa."

Nan's logic seemed off somehow, but I still took another cookie. Anyway, the earrings were going to do it all. "When's supper, anyway?"

"Well, we're on our own tonight. Your mom's working on an offer and Patricia's shift ends at nine."

"Is this the night Patricia's doing the security for the grand opening at Economart?"

"Yup. She's pretty nervous about it. They're expecting a big turnout."

"You know what?" I went for the lunch in my backpack. "Never mind about supper for me then. I didn't eat all of my sandwich today. I'll have that and get over to Andrea's."

"Are you sure? You're a growing girl. You need your energy."

"I'll be fine." I bit into the slightly soggy egg-salad sandwich. Even after reverse chocolate chip it tasted great.

Nan and I watched together as Mr. and Ms Butterscotch sold an orthopaedic back rest, special wrist weights and a foot massager. By that time the whole plate of cookies was gone. "I'm going to call Mom. I want to take the video camera to Andrea's." I dialled up the Regal Trust office and left a message to page Mom. She called me back after a couple of minutes and I could tell by the background noise, that sishing sound, that she was in the car.

"Hello, Lauren. Brenda and I are presenting an

offer in half an hour, so I can only talk for a minute. Did we get a letter from your father today?"

"No, at least Nan didn't mention it. Mom, I want to borrow the camcorder, okay?"

"You're not making more horror movies with Stephanie, are you? I had to pick dried ketchup off the lens the last time."

"No. I'm helping Andrea with a presentation."

"Is she coming to our house?"

"No, she's baby-sitting Noah and Neil."

Mom sighed. Working with Andrea's mom so closely, she understood how hard baby–sitting the twins could be. "All right. But don't let the twins touch the camera."

"Bye, Mom."

"Love you," she said and hung up.

"The cookies were great, Nan." I piled my lunch containers on top of the cookie plate and took it back into the kitchen. Then I grabbed the camera bag from Mom's office.

"Take a jacket. Temperature's dropping. I heard it on the weather channel," Nan warned.

"Maybe in the Yukon," I teased. "C'mon Nan, next Monday's the official first day of spring."

"So take an umbrella too."

"Yeah, sure, whatever," I said, but I did slip on my lumber jacket to make her happy. "I'll see you later."

"There's a good girl." Nan kissed my cheek and saw me out the door.

With my stomach full of Nan's delicious cookies, I felt happy in spite of going to Andrea's house. The sunshine at this hour of the day was a real treat and so warm on my shoulders that I peeled off my jacket.

Andrea's doorbell sounded a programmed *William Tell Overture* when I pushed the button. From inside I heard doors slamming, footsteps pounding and happy shrieking.

The door opened. Andrea wiped a sweaty strand of hair from her face. "Oh, hi," she said breathlessly. "Mom's still not home. Could you just take your shoes off?"

"I heard they're presenting an offer," I told Andrea as I bent down to pull off my sneakers. From where I stood I could see her room through the open door. It looked amazingly perfect, her bed smooth, the dust ruffle hanging straight, the floor around it clear, with no dust bunnies or old food. "Your mom won't be back for a while. Where's your stepdad?"

"Roy's probably running late too. Guess I'd better make supper for the twins." Andrea shut the door to her room as we headed for the kitchen. "Macaroni and cheese will be quick," she said, still slightly out of breath from rushing around. She banged a potful of water onto the stove.

"Listen, Andrea. I saw your cue cards. Your notes looked great. Why don't you just tell me your speech while you're fixing supper."

"Oh, I'd feel stupid," she said as she reached into the cupboard for the macaroni.

"That's the point. The stupider you feel when you practise, the more normal you feel when you're in front of the class."

"All right, if you really think so." She started her speech as she hunted for the butter in the fridge. "I want to be a veterinarian in an equine practice because I love horses . . . "

"Why?"

"Hmm." Andrea shut the fridge door and stood in front of it. "I guess it's because horses are strong but really gentle. And they have friendly eyes."

"Friendly eyes?" I repeated.

"Uh huh. Horses look at you as though they like you no matter what. Their eyes don't judge. They just accept."

Andrea spoke quicker now. "And horses obey you. They take you places you can't go. And when you're riding, you feel like they're part of you. You're working together with your horse and . . . and you become stronger." Andrea's eyes shone now. "It's really hard to explain."

"Do you have a favourite breed?"

"Arabians, definitely. The horse I ride at the Triple–R is half Arabian and half quarter horse. He's so smart. You wouldn't believe it. He once pulled a carrot from my back pocket, and now every time I visit I keep one there and he always looks for it. My dream is to own and breed Arabians, and I'll be able to treat them myself after veterinary school. Or if that doesn't work out, I'll find a job at the race-track. As long as I'm around horses."

Andrea rushed the words out so breathlessly that even though I'd always thought horses were just big and smelly, she made me excited about them, made me want to ride too.

I clicked on the camcorder and started filming.

"But I'm only telling *you*." Andrea raised her hand to block the lens. "This is just for practice."

"Just tell me everything you said all over again."

She did, and forgot to stir the macaroni. Noah dashed through as she poured it into a sieve.

"Yuck. It's all stuck together. Mommy never makes it that way."

"Mom never makes it at all, you little dweeb." She grabbed him and planted a kiss on his cheek. "Get Neil, please." Andrea lopped off a hunk of butter and stirred it into the macaroni. Then she shook half a container of dried orange cheese into the pot. "You having some, Lauren?"

"I shouldn't, I'm — " 'Dieting' was the word I didn't say. How could I when Andrea was a good size bigger than I was? She doled herself a large bowlful. "Sure I'll have some," I answered. Just this once, so I wouldn't hurt her feelings. The earrings, EZ-Slims, they'll do the trick. Thirty-day money-back guarantee.

Neil and Noah scoffed the macaroni down, but

before they could tear off, Andrea brought out some chocolate pudding. "Want some, Lauren?" she asked.

I felt really stuffed. "None for me, thanks." I really didn't need any, but as I watched Andrea spoon some into dessert dishes and then top it with spray-can whipped cream, I felt left out. Andrea brought out candy sprinkles and a jar of green cherries.

"Aw, Andy, you're the bestest," Neil said as she helped him and Noah turn their pudding into something irresistible.

Still I resisted. None for me — is that what being thin was all about? I noticed Andrea didn't take any for herself either.

Andrea wiped off the twins' faces.

"Can I help?" I asked as she rinsed off the dishes.

"Well, Mom likes the dishwasher loaded a certain way. Makes it much easier to unload. Do you want to sweep the floor?"

"Sure," I said, though the floor looked perfect already.

"You missed a macaroni there." Andrea pointed underneath Neil's chair.

I swept up the macaroni. It's what I hated about being at Andrea's house: her fussing to have everything clean and perfect for her mother, and the twins tearing around pulling it all apart again. Andrea never seemed to relax, even in her own house.

"Let's watch the video now," I suggested.

"Okay. I just have to get the twins to give up the TV. Neil! Noah!" she called as we went into the family room. "We need to use the VCR for a minute. It's for school. I'll pay you a dollar," she offered.

"Two dollars!" Noah demanded.

"I wanna make a movie!" Neil said.

I ignored them both, switched the TV to channel three and plugged the camcorder wire into the back. By that time Andrea's stepdad walked in. We heard him clanking out ice cubes into a glass.

"Daddy, Daddy!" Neil and Noah shrieked. As he stepped into the family room they grabbed hold of either side of him with such force that he almost fell.

"Hi. What's going on?" he asked as he loosened his tie. A twin clinging to each leg, he shuffled closer to a couch. The ice cubes in his Coke crackled. "Hey, let go, let go! Watch my drink! Andrea?"

"Let your dad sit down," Andrea told Neil and Noah, grabbing each by an arm.

"Thanks, Andy." Roy smiled and slid onto the sofa.

Andrea released the twins and they curled up on either side of their father.

"We're about to watch a tape of Andrea's school presentation," I told Roy, in case the twins wanted to insist on cartoons. Then I pressed PLAY on the camcorder.

Roy watched silently, sipping at his Coke. The twins pointed and giggled.

"You see, Andrea, you're great," I said at the end of her speech. "All you have to do is be yourself in front of the class and tell them exactly what you did on the tape."

"Easy for you to say." She knelt beside me, her arms crossed. "Even Mom thinks you're amazing. Since you played The Great Lakes in that environmental play last year, she says you have charisma." Andrea shook her head and frowned. "But me — I don't know. You saw what happens. I get shaky and fumbly. I drop my cue cards."

"Don't take them up then. You know your speech by heart." I rewound a bit of the tape and played it. "See there, you're looking at me. That's good. Make eye contact."

"You know, she's right, Andy," Roy said, his mouth twisting up at the corners, not quite a smile.

Andrea unfolded her arms and turned to face him. "I hate seeing them all sitting in their chairs watching me. I know what they're all thinking." She pushed her hair behind her ears. " 'No wonder Andrea likes horses, she's as big as one.' They don't listen to what I say. They just pick apart what I look like."

"We–ll," Roy took a long sip from his glass. "To me you're perfect just the way you are but if it bothers you so much . . . Well . . . " He went on uncomfortably. "Have you ever thought of maybe trying to lose some weight?"

It wasn't exactly a radical idea. The whinnying and snorting from the boys, and Kim's insults, all sent out that same message. I glanced at Andrea to see how she was going to take the suggestion from Roy.

Andrea's mouth and cheeks sagged, she bit at her lip.

"Don't look like that," Roy said. "Up till now I never said anything. You were a little girl. It was just baby fat. But now you're a young woman. And if you think it's affecting your life . . . "

Andrea stood up and ran from the room.

And just like Ms Smyrnios, Roy didn't chase after her. He looked like he didn't know what to do, just sighed and sipped at his drink. Nobody said anything for a few moments. Even the twins stayed quiet, Noah sucking two middle fingers, Neil sucking his thumb.

"Well, I guess I should be going," I said as I unplugged the camcorder and placed it back in the bag. Roy shrugged sort of helplessly.

Neil stood on the couch and wrapped his arms around Roy's neck. I noticed his arms were slim and dark like his dad's — no baby fat there. And in a bratty kind of way, yeah, he and his brother were pretty cute. Cuter than a chunky teenager anyway. Maybe that's why Andrea never relaxed.

I swung the bag over my shoulder. "Bye Neil, bye Noah."

They shrieked and chortled but didn't seem to notice me slipping out. On the way to the front door I had to pass Andrea's room. I couldn't just leave without saying anything to her, although I didn't really know what I could say. I took a deep breath and knocked softly. "Andrea?"

"Come in."

I eased the door open. Andrea sat on her bed facing her mirror, staring. A poster of a black stallion rearing up on his back legs was reflected beside her in the mirror. In her hands she held a picture of a man I only vaguely remembered. Her dad. He'd given piggyback rides at Andrea's sixth birthday, but some time after the big split he moved to Vancouver. I looked at him closely. Large blue eyes, round pink cheeks and a soft chin — he looked a lot like Andrea.

"He's fat, and my mother dumped him years ago," she said.

"Aw, come off it," I said. "That had nothing to do with it. You said they were always fighting."

"Yes," she said as she placed her father's picture back on her dresser. "But Roy's right. Being fat does affect your life. If I could lose weight, everything would be perfect."

What could I say? You're not even a quarter of the size of the piano-case lady in *The Sun*. I tried that out inside my head, but it didn't sound helpful. "Look Andrea, you have to learn not to care so much about what other people think. You start your speech, the morons at the back snicker, you ignore them. If you let them rattle you, they'll only keep it up." It was my sister's "Don't let them see that it hurts" speech, only I couldn't tell from Andrea's face whether it was sinking in. "And as far as what Roy said," I added, "you gotta know by now that parents suffer from hoof-in-the-mouth disease."

Andrea wiped away a tear.

Aw, gees . . . I kept talking. "Anyway, I'm dieting. Jay Friessen thinks I'd be a knockout if I were thinner. Maybe I'll be a knockout in time for the public speaking competition." I watched another tear land on her hand. I tried to say something to make her feel better. "You've got great blond hair and your skin is always so clear. Stephanie gets huge zits on her nose sometimes."

Andrea didn't even seem to hear me. She bunched her hands into fists. She seemed to be somewhere far away, an angry bitter place, rearing up like that stallion. "I'll show him." She punched the bed. "I'll show them. I'll lose so much weight I *will* be perfect."

Chapter 3

Andrea presented her speech the next day. As I suggested, she didn't take up her cue cards. Instead she wrote the key points on her hands. Every once in a while she glanced down at them, which made her look like she was praying. The only eye contact she made was with me.

I put my fingers to the corners of my lips and pulled them into a grin, hoping she'd take the hint and smile. She did, but it was a startled, flashbulb kind of smile. I couldn't feel her excitement this time, not like last night, but she made it through the speech and I gave her an A+ on my evaluation.

"Another A for Andrea," Stephanie grumbled to me at lunch. "As if she needs it. You never helped me with my presentation." She eyed the four reverse chocolate chip cookies in the centre of the table at lunch, my peace offering for passing up on "Frankenbeast." She placed a bag of tortilla chips next to them. Hers for being annoyed.

"You never asked, Steph." I shrugged my shoulders. "Besides it wasn't important to you. You threw your speech together the night before."

"Okay, so I'm not Miss Start-it-the-night-it's-assigned like Andrea." Stephanie took a cookie. "You aren't either."

"True." I grinned. "Make you a deal. We'll both start way earlier on our May speech. That way I can help you."

"And you'll have it really together for the Halton competition in June. Have some chips."

Tortilla chips. Would eating a handful be fattening? I stuffed some in my mouth. "Anyway, just to let you know, Andrea wrote her own speech. All I did was give her a pep talk." I stared at the cookies now. Nan had said they weren't junk food. I picked one up.

Behind me I heard a rustle.

"Have a seat, Andrea, please," Stephanie suggested, a little crook in her mouth.

"Thank you." Andrea pulled back a metal chair and lowered herself onto it. Then she took a plastic container from her bag and flipped off the lid. Four sticks of celery, four carrots. "I'm on a diet," she explained as she crunched into a carrot. *Snap, crunch, snap, crunch.* Andrea's food sounded angry.

I ate my sandwich and reached for a cookie before I noticed Andrea hadn't taken anything else out of her bag. She sat with her hands locked together in front of her on the table. "That can't be all you're eating, Andrea. Have a cookie." I set the one in my hand down near her.

"No!" she answered like the crack of her celery. "I'm dieting, I told you." She pushed the reverse chocolate chip back in front of me. Her face flushed red and then turned her normal pink again. "I still have an apple anyway." She took it out and bit into it.

I tried to make one cookie last as long as Andrea's vegetables had, sucking at the crumbs in my mouth, savouring the chocolate. What if Andrea really meant it? What if she stuck to a diet and became thinner than I was? By the time the first lunch bell rang, I'd eaten the second cookie too. Meanwhile Andrea annihilated the apple. She barely had a core to throw away.

"She must be starving," Stephanie whispered at me when Andrea took off to the library to look up some horse disease.

"Yeah, what willpower."

"C'mon, one day she's eating fries. The next, she's eating nothing. She always goes way overboard." Steph rolled her eyes. "And she can't possibly keep it up, right? She'll probably stuff herself tonight."

"Yeah, probably." But I remembered Andrea looking in the mirror yesterday and vowing to lose so much weight she'd be perfect. Perfect like her room, perfect like her grades, perfect like the floor in her kitchen — if she could control all those things, maybe she could control her weight too.

I thought my goal of becoming a knockout was

much more realistic. "I need to diet too, Steph. For the Halton Public Speaking Competition — I just have to be thin."

"I don't see why. But you know, Kim was telling me about this sure-fire diet. Have you ever tried those rice cake thingies?"

"No. Are they any good?"

"I don't know. But Kim's cousin in Alberta weighed over two hundred pounds. Then she ate nothing but rice cakes for a couple of months and now she's slim."

"Really?"

"Well, Kim says so anyway. I usually take everything she says with a box of salt." Stephanie shrugged. "Honest, Lauren, you don't need to lose weight for the competition. You're a great speaker."

"Hmm. The competition's in three months, I'd have enough time. Rice cakes, eh?"

"Yeah, they kind of sound desserty, don't you think? You'd have to take vitamin pills, to stay healthy and all."

"Sure, I could do that, couldn't I?"

But how would I be able to handle Nanna? She thought her cookies were health food, so how would she feel about her suppers? Well, I'd worry about that later.

Stephanie stopped at the grocery store with me on the way home. At first we couldn't find the rice cakes.

"Oh, they wouldn't be in the bakery department." The cashier smiled at us and pointed. "They're down aisle eight, left-hand side, above the oatmeal."

"Thanks." We walked toward where she pointed and found bags of rice cakes just where she said they would be.

"Hey, are they ever light," Stephanie said as she passed me a package. "Sort of like styrofoam, eh?"

"I guess," I answered as we headed for the cash to pay. I pocketed my change and we continued walking home, me with a new springiness to my step now that I had the answer to my weight problem in my bag.

Nanna offered me some homemade banana bread when we got home. "None for me," I told her. "I'm trying out a new snack."

Stephanie grabbed a slice of Nan's bread and buttered it.

"Want to try one of these, too?" I asked, holding out one of the rice cakes. Airy like a feather. Yeah, I guess it *did* feel like styrofoam.

"Sure, I'll try anything." Stephanie took the puck-shaped cake and bit into it. When her teeth connected it sounded like dry wood cracking, or maybe like that old chair snapping beneath me in class.

I bit into one — more wood cracked — and chewed. Crunchy and dry. "Hmm. It tastes like . . . um, what does this remind me of? Sugar Crisp."

"Without the sugar," Stephanie agreed.

"Or maybe saltines," I continued.

"Without the salt," Stephanie added.

"Or corn flakes."

This time both of us spoke at the same time. "Without the corn!" We broke up.

"Let me try one of your new snacks." Nan cracked into a cake now. "Something is missing. It needs something." She picked up the package. "Yup, look here. It says 'Enjoy with your favourite spreads, cheeses, cold cuts, pizza toppings.' You can't eat these things plain. Why, without anything on top, they taste like styrofoam."

Felt like and tasted like. We broke up again. But could I last a whole month eating only styrofoam? I thought of Jay. I'd be a knockout for him. I'd deliver my May presentation and he would fall deeply in love with me when he saw me up there all thin and beautiful. I thought of Andrea eating her carrots and celery. I can do it, I *know* I can do it, I told myself.

That's when Patricia came in carrying a couple of big brown paper bags. My sister has a strong, square face but all the corners on it seemed to round as she smiled at me. A warm spicy beef-and-noodley smell wafted around her.

"I'm celebrating," she announced as she placed the packages on the table. "Chinese. There's tons, Stephanie. You can stay." Patricia looked happy as she rinsed off her hands under the kitchen taps and began to set the table.

"Allll right! I love Chinese!" Stephanie said.

"You didn't get accepted by the Halton Police Board, did you?" I asked. Patricia had flunked with two other boards but for the Halton test Mom had worked with her, reviewing old grammar books and even studying "It Pays To Increase Your Word Power" in *Reader's Digest*.

"I would have seen a letter from them in the mail," Nan answered. "We did get a postcard from your father though."

"Oh yeah?" Patricia asked. "What did he say?"

"Patricia, we want to know about your good news!" I grabbed the cutlery from her hand and continued setting the table so she could stay focussed.

"Yeah," Stephanie agreed. "C'mon, what gives?"

"Today I caught a shoplifter and made him cry." Patricia's smile stretched wider.

"What! You made someone cry and that makes your day?" I stared at her.

"Did you give him a big karate chop?" Stephanie asked, leaning forward as though she expected a demonstration.

"Steph, she takes judo, not karate," I cut in. "Did you put a choke hold on him?" I asked. I knew that was Patricia's favourite move.

"Let Patricia tell us the story her own way," Nan told us.

"Should we wait for Mom?" Patricia asked as she opened a container. "Or is she coming later?"

"Later," Nan swished her hand in the air, just as impatient as Stephanie and I were to hear the story. "Who was the person you caught?"

"Let me see. His name was Gerald — um — Asten or Ashbrook, or was it Elton? Anyhow the guys all call him Sport."

"You have a name for this shoplifter?" Nan asked.

"Yeah, he comes in a lot. But he was wearing a bulky parka and it wasn't that cold out today. I followed him around."

"And?" Stephanie prodded.

"Well, he pushed around a shopping cart and bought a hunting vest and some knives. But I noticed he pocketed a couple of fishing lures."

"So he paid for some of the stuff?" I asked.

"And stole the lures. I saw him. There was no doubt in my mind." Patricia shook her head. "None. So I followed him out of the store and asked if he would empty his pockets."

"Did he pull one of the hunting knives on you?" Stephanie craned forward again.

Patricia shook her head.

"What did he have to say for himself?" Nan asked.

"He said it was all a mistake. He had just put them in his pocket so they wouldn't get caught on the vest in the carriage. And then he forgot."

"And you wouldn't let him off?" It was the hard side of my sister showing itself, and I could never quite understand it.

"No. He begged me. He even offered money." Patricia beamed now. "That's when he started to cry."

"Why are we celebrating this?" Nan asked.

"Jock said it's the last trick of the shoplifter, crying. If you get them to that stage, you've beat them."

"What if it really was a mistake? People forget all the time," Nan said.

"People lie all the time, too. We've been watching Sport for a while, only today . . . " Patricia pointed at herself proudly, "I caught him."

"Yeah, but it's only a fishing lure," I told her.

"Stealing is stealing." Patricia shook her head as she repeated the line. It sounded like something someone else had told her and now she believed it, which is exactly like Patricia. "It doesn't matter how small the theft is, if we catch the shoplifter with the goods, Jock prosecutes. Anyway, Jock promoted me. No more pretend shopping for me. I'm going to be a uniformed security guard."

"That's great, Patricia!" Stephanie told her.

"A uniform," she sighed to herself, and beamed. She started dishing out the fried rice.

Fried rice or rice cakes — gee, this was tough. I

resisted for a fraction of a second and then decided tomorrow was a better day to start dieting. I grabbed a couple of egg rolls and some plum sauce. I dipped one in the sauce and tore into it. Boy, nothing tastes as good as forbidden food.

"Did Jock give you a raise?" Nan asked.

Patricia scooped out some chow mein from a tub and then stopped to look at Nan. "A raise?" Some of the squareness returned to her face.

"Yes, if it's a promotion you usually get more money."

"Well . . . I get a free uniform."

"Don't let him take advantage of you, Patricia," Nan warned. "You work hard and you deserve an increase."

"He said in three months, when I get the routine down."

"Uh-huh." Nan didn't have to say more. The way she reset her purple glasses back close against her nose said it all. In three months Jock had better give Patricia a raise.

"Where's Dad's postcard?" I asked to try to get the happy floating feeling back in the air.

"Over on the counter near the microwave."

A stack of mail lay there. I noticed an oversized postcard, but it wasn't from Dad. One side showed a woman relaxing in a whirlpool. "Select Women's Spa and Fitness Centre," the caption read. And on the flip side: "Results guaranteed, lose inches fast!

Scratch here to see if you have won a prize."

With my thumb nail I scraped off the grey coating. *Congratulations! You have won a free* one-year membership. Call immediately to claim your prize.* I read the tiny print at the bottom: **Subject to monthly registration fee of \$12.00 payable at time of joining.*

I flipped it over again and pictured myself in the whirlpool. Could that work? It would use up almost all my allowance. If the rice cakes and earrings didn't make me lose weight in the next month, I'd still have time to try this health club. I laid the card beside the microwave again and shuffled through the rest of the mail.

"Here it is!" I called. "Hey, Taj Mahal! Awesome. Says here 'India's another world. Be glad you're growing up in Canada. We're way behind on our installation schedule. The systems won't be fully operational till next spring. You'll have to visit at least once. Maybe in the summer holidays if the heat's not too bad. Otherwise pick a country and we can meet there. Love, Dad.'"

"Next spring!" Patricia repeated. For a second her smile sagged, and then it disappeared.

"Don't think about how long he'll be away, Patricia. Think about visiting India," Nan said brightly — a little too brightly.

"Wow, India," Steph repeated.

Patricia's face became square and strong again.

She nodded. "I don't know when I can take my vacation."

At that moment the front door crashed open. "I'm home," my mother called. "Come on everybody! Grab your coats, we're going out for dinner to celebrate. The Simmonses accepted the offer on their house." By the time she reached the end of her sentence, she also reached the end of the hall into the kitchen. "Oh, you're eating," she said softly. She took off her coat now and draped it over Dad's chair. "Hi, Stephanie."

"Hi, Mrs. Dreyburgh. We're already celebrating."

"Patricia's been promoted," Nan told Mom. "She brought home Chinese."

"Jock made me a uniformed security guard." Patricia smiled again.

"And you got a raise! That's wonderful, Patricia."

"No, Mom. I got a uniform."

"Well . . . well, that's good." Mom sat down. "This is terrific, Patricia," she said as she helped herself to some chow mein.

"Dad's not coming home ever," Patricia blurted out.

"Now where did you get that idea?"

"In the postcard. They won't finish installing till next year!"

Mom put down her fork and stood up, frowning. "I'm getting some water. Anybody else for a glass?"

"Me," I told her.

She stood with her back to us for a long time, rinsing out the water pitcher, then filling it up. By the time she brought the glasses and pitcher to the table, the water had already seeped through the filter. "It's too bad about your father. But tonight is a celebration for both of us, Patricia. And we can't let one piece of bad news spoil it." She poured herself a glass of water now and sipped. "I know, you got the Chinese, so why don't I take us all out for ice cream after?"

"Great," Stephanie agreed.

The idea cheered everyone up again. And Mom didn't just buy us cones either. She splurged. "The works," she offered as we lined up to choose.

So of course Steph and I ordered chocolate-dip waffle cones complete with sprinkles and double scoops of Death by Chocolate. Tomorrow, I told myself. Tomorrow, I would start again trying to become a knockout.

Chapter 4

"Breakfast is the most important meal of the day," Nan told me next morning when I tried to get away with eating only a rice cake. "Have some pancakes. Just don't butter them."

I love pancakes and never butter them, but as usual I poured on a lake of syrup. Lunch is when I'll start, I thought. I'll have rice cakes for lunch.

But by eleven o'clock the hall near the cafeteria filled with a warm tomato beefy smell. I sniffed the air. "Lasagna," I muttered to Stephanie. "My favourite."

We sat down at our regular spot. I unwrapped my styrofoam puck and bit into it. *Crack!* Puffed rice crumbled onto the table. I couldn't do it. I couldn't be satisfied with the rice cakes when lasagna beckoned to me from just beyond the next table.

I felt out of control, like the video-game character chasing Frankenbeast. My legs carried me quickly to the line-up. I shot forward to where the lasagna was and nodded to Mrs. Fatawa as she slid a large helping onto my plate. I shot forward again to pay and then beamed back to my table. Andrea was just setting down her backpack on the floor next to my chair.

I felt weak and guilty as my teeth sank into the soft cheesey layers. Especially when Andrea snapped into her carrots and celery. But I continued to eat — a video character consuming everything in its path. When I finally put my fork down the plate looked clean, licked clean.

"Here," Stephanie said, tossing a package of cupcakes across the table. "Mom bought your favourite."

They landed, plunk, in front of me. I couldn't help picking them up, holding them, turning them around, studying them. Chocolate icing with white icing squiggles decorating the top. And in the centre of that fudgey chocolate, I knew, rested a pocket of white creamy filling.

Andrea glanced down at the package. Her nose twitched. Too many carrots — she was turning into a rabbit. Or maybe a horse. Then the twitch turned into a wrinkle and she raised her eyebrows. Andrea, the heaviest girl in grade seven, was wrinkling her nose and raising her eyebrows at my dessert!

"None for me, thanks." I forced a smile for Stephanie as I pushed the package back to her. With Andrea sticking so well to her rabbit food, I needed to show some willpower. But saying no to those cupcakes made me feel unsatisfied. My teeth and eyebrows itched, I wanted to stand up and sit down, to run back and forth and around the table. I wanted to snatch back that package, rip it open and eat it before any part of my body could realize what I was doing and tell me, No, no, Lauren! I wanted Andrea to stop raising her eyebrows and go back to eating regular food again.

This was impossible! I poked a hole into another styrofoam puck with my finger. There sat Stephanie, thin as Nan's broomstick, eating everything in sight. Andrea, solid as a block, crunching celery sticks. And me, wanting to be thin . . . wanting to eat . . . wanting to be thin . . . wanting to eat . . .

Andrea didn't even finish her vegetables. "You'll excuse me," she pushed away from the table and stood up. "I have some work to do in the library."

"I think you should eat your vegetables first," Stephanie teased.

"Bye." I smiled as she walked away.

"Guess what, Lauren," Kim's bright voice called to me as Andrea stepped out the cafeteria door. She slunk over to our table from the cafeteria line, her thick red hair bouncing along her shoulders. "Do you know they've decided to add a cash prize to the Halton Public Speaking Competition? One hundred dollars. Mom took notes for the meeting yesterday."

Before that had a chance to sink in my heart

seized. There close behind Kim, with his hand owning her hip, stood Jay!

"Uh — um — " I stammered.

"You get that huge trophy and one hundred dollars. My father still remembers when you were the ringmaster for that circus thing we did in grade two. He thinks you're a natural." She buttered on a little smile. "How about you, Jay? What do you think?"

She stood to one side so I could see his arm stretching around her back.

Jay grinned, raised one thumb and winked.

"Well, I just thought you'd want to know." Again Kim smiled and I knew she was letting me know about something more than the prize. Before I could answer, the two of them sauntered away.

"He winked at you," Stephanie said. "Did you see? He winked at you."

"Yeah, but he was holding her." Inside, my heart sagged like a broken chair.

"Come on, she has the personality of a . . . "

"Rice cake?" I suggested.

"That's it. All you have to do is — "

"Lose weight, I know. I'd be a knockout."

"I was thinking of the *contest*, Lauren. Just come up with a good topic. Everybody loves your speeches. Jay always laughs. He's got to like you better than the human rice cake. If he has any taste."

"A good topic, huh! The only thing I can think about lately is food."

"That could work. You can talk about all the different diets you've heard about."

"Not if I'm this size. And I don't know if I can lose weight."

"Not that you need to," Steph started diplomatically, raising her eyebrows and one finger, "but if you really set your mind to it, you could do anything."

After school we rented "Frankenbeast" at full price and Stephanie and I played it at her house. She nuked a large bowl of nachos so that the cheddar cheese melted in long strings over the chips. She also mixed some cream cheese and salsa for dip. "Mmm. Have some." She pushed the bowl toward me.

"Stephanie, remember losing weight? Really setting my mind to it?" I said, sniffing the cheddar.

She pulled the bowl back. "Oh, sorry, I forgot. I'm starving. You don't mind if I eat some?"

"No, that's okay, I'm developing willpower." And I thought I was too. Until Frankenbeast ripped off the head of my video body. Then without even thinking I stuffed a handful of chips into my mouth. Stephanie didn't seem to notice.

That night Nan made fried chicken with cow-chips and caesar salad — my favourite. I only ate one helping. It nearly made me cry, but I turned down dessert too, Nan's homemade nanaimo bars. Of the three that appeared in my lunch the next day, I only ate one.

When I stepped onto the scale on Saturday, I'd gained three pounds. I felt pretty bad about that till Steph came over and we started filming a magic show with Mom's video camera.

"I'll lie down on the couch with my eyes closed. How do I look?" she asked.

"Fold your arms across your chest. That's good." I twisted a towel around my head for a turban and threw another one around my shoulders for a cape. "Okay, I'm starting the camera," I said as I pressed the remote. "And now I, the Amazing Swami, will make this body disappear." I waved my hands over Stephanie, and chanted the first rhyming words that came to my mind:

Chocolate doughnuts, apple pie.
Take this body to the sky.

Then I stopped the camera. "Okay, get up now."

She scrambled out of the camera's view so the finished video would show just a blank where her body had been. I pressed START again and gestured to the empty couch, bowing. "I am truly amazing."

By Monday, I'd lost two of the three pounds again.

By Wednesday I was up three. Stephanie and I started making a new video. We filmed Patricia's stuffed Leo the Lobster "crawling" across the floor by painstakingly stopping the camera, moving Leo, and starting the camera over and over again. Snacking only on rice cakes the rest of the week, I managed to lose the four pounds I'd put on.

Where were my earrings?

The week after that the stores started displaying all their Easter stuff and selling my favourite miniature caramel eggs. I didn't even try to diet. Stephanie and I each ate about six while finishing "Attack of the Killer Lobster."

Every day I searched the mail for my earrings. They were my only hope. And every lunch hour Andrea turned down my offers of chocolate bunny parts, and continued nibbling on carrots and celery, which made me feel worse.

"Lauren," Kim asked me, pointing out the window during homeroom one morning, "that can't be Andrea's mom, can it?"

"Who else?" I said when I saw the hunter-green T-bird parked out front. But I understood what she meant when Andrea stepped out of the passenger side and stood beside her mom. It had never struck me how tiny Mrs. Partington was until then. "Brenda only wears a size five," Mom had told me once, with envy in her voice. She'd also told me about how Mrs. Partington owned a matching pair of shoes for every outfit and how the first Monday of every month was reserved for her hairdressing appointment.

"Andrea looks like a house next to her mom," Kim said.

I frowned. Kim was as diplomatic as a tank. But Andrea stuck out in all kinds of ways, not just her size. She didn't rush away from her mother the way a normal kid would. Instead she smiled and seemed to be listening in awe to what Mrs. Partington was telling her. Then Andrea kissed her mom goodbye, which really seemed bizarre. Where most grade sevens ducked their parents' kisses, Andrea actually wanted her mom's.

The following Monday — three weeks of eating celery and carrots later — Andrea dashed in late for homeroom wearing a tight white T-shirt tucked into a pair of jogging pants. SELECT WOMEN FITNESS the slightly stretched words across her chest read.

Ms Smyrnios called her to the front to pick up a corrected math sheet. As Andrea wandered back to her seat, looking the sheet over, a warm queasy feeling grabbed at my stomach. Andrea's waist had shrunk. Without her usual shape-hiding dress I could see that her body went in and out instead of just out and down the way it used to. *Is she fatter than I am?* I played the game and realized that soon *I* might be losing.

"You look nice today," Ms Smyrnios called after her.

Andrea dipped her head and sat down quickly, all pink and embarrassed as usual.

"Looking fit, Andrea," Ms Bryant, our gym teacher, commented later.

"Did you lose some weight?" Emily asked her at lunchtime on our way to the cafeteria.

"Ten pounds," Andrea murmured.

"Andrea's hot!" Jay whispered loudly, making a gesture with his hands that showed he liked where her body went out.

Andrea turned away from him. Her skin colour changed from pink to plum.

Kim sneered. "Kind of like taking a cup of water from the ocean if you ask me," she muttered as she headed off.

I don't know how she did it, but Andrea managed to act like she hadn't heard.

"You should wear more clothes like that," Stephanie suggested as we sat down to lunch.

"I hate this T-shirt," Andrea snapped. Her celery and carrots sat there untouched.

"So okay, the Select Women part is pretty dumb," I said. "But I think Stephanie means it fits you and shows off — "

"It's disgusting. I stick out." Andrea shut her eyes for a moment as if to close the shirt from her mind.

"Aw, don't pay any attention to what Jay says.

He's just a sleazebucket," Stephanie told her. "A cute sleazebucket, though." She sighed and smiled for my benefit.

"I don't care about him. But the T-shirt looks gross on me. I hate it."

"Then why'd you wear it?" I was suddenly tired of everyone paying so much attention to Andrea. "I've never seen it on you before."

"It's my mother's. When she drove me to school this morning we were rear-ended by a truck and her coffee splashed all over my dress. She lent me this from her gym bag."

"So now you fit your mother's clothes?" I asked.

"It's humongous on her." Andrea tugged the T-shirt away from her body. "And way too tight for me." She took off suddenly and returned with some cutlery from the cafeteria tray.

Sitting there watching her take a plastic container of veggies from her bag, I still wanted to eat everything in sight — Patricia's liverwurst sandwich that Nan had accidentally given me, Stephanie's ketchup chips, my banana muffin. The french fries with brown gravy on Carlos's plate next table over. The boston cream pie behind the glass-plated section of the cafeteria line . . . I felt a gnawing dislike for Andrea.

"How do you do it?" I asked, watching as she took out only one celery stick and snapped the lid back on her container.

"Do you really want to know?" She laid down her stick of celery.

"Yeah, sure. I wanna lose weight too."

"Okay. I skip breakfast." Andrea cut her celery into four pieces.

"Nan would never let me do that." I shook my head. Andrea wasn't telling me what I really needed to know.

"Mom's too busy getting the twins ready for preschool to notice. I tell her I'm having a Nutribar." She shrugged her shoulders and continued. "Then I have celery and carrots and an apple for lunch. And for supper I eat salad and maybe some potato. But no meat. It has too much fat."

"But how can you not eat more?" I howled in frustration. When heads turned to look at me, I repeated the question in a desperate whisper, "How do you do it?" My hand curled over my muffin.

"I keep remembering my father," Andrea replied.

"You mean what he said about being fat affecting your life?"

"Roy said that. No, I mean my real father. I don't want to end up looking like him." She finished her celery and folded her hands in front of her.

"Andrea, aren't you eating your carrots and apple?" Stephanie asked.

"No, I'm not really hungry."

Stephanie gave me her zombie-at-midnight

stare and I knew why. Andrea was getting weird about her food. But I didn't care. All I knew was that she was winning the losing game, and forcing me to play harder too.

After school Stephanie came to my house. Nan greeted us with a plate of brownies.

"Do you always have to make fattening foods!" I snapped at her.

"I thought you liked my brownies. I . . . I'll just put them away."

"Wait, wait!" Stephanie grabbed a couple before Nan could walk away.

"Do you want me to cut up some fruit for you, Lauren?" Nan asked.

"No, I don't want anything!" I could see her back go stiff. I hadn't really meant to yell like that.

Nan turned to face me again, her wrinkles joining into a frown. She pointed to the counter beside the microwave. "That package is for you."

I snatched up a small brown padded envelope. THE SHOPPING NETWORK, the bold letters of the return address read. "My earrings!" I shouted. "They're finally here." With shaking hands I tore open the end flap and fumbled with a tiny white box. Three weeks of waiting and now the answer to my prayers was here.

"Hey, they're okay," Stephanie said when I took the earrings off their velvet backing. We went to the mirror in the bathroom and I followed the instructions to put them on.

"I don't know if I've done this right," I told Stephanie after screwing the backs against my ear lobes. "They feel awfully tight."

"I don't see how else you could do it. You probably just have to get used to them."

"Yeah. Well, I'll force myself. Anything to lose weight like Andrea." I pictured her in that Select Women T-shirt again. "Do you think if I lose weight I'll look bigger — you know, on top — like Andrea?"

"Don't you want to be slimmer?" Stephanie asked.

"I don't know. I want Jay to like me." I thought for a while. "Probably I'd like to have long skinny legs and arms, a tiny waist and big boobs."

"A Barbie doll."

"What?"

"You want to look like a Barbie doll. Well, I guess I'd like a little shape too." Stephanie glanced down at her T-shirt and frowned. "Hey, that gives me an idea."

"What?"

"Do you still have your Barbie dolls?"

"Yeah, in the toybox in the crawl space."

"Great. How about we get them and make a movie?"

"Will Barbie be the victim of some terrible monster?" My ear lobes pulsed hot against my new earrings.

Stephanie grinned. "I hadn't thought about it!"

"Will I need ketchup?" I asked, trying to move one earring slightly so it wouldn't feel so tight.

"I like the way you're thinking."

"All right. But we have to be careful not to get any on the camcorder this time."

Chapter 5

"That's it, Lauren. You're not reading any more Horror Hall books." Mom's nyloned feet had sneak-sneaked along the plush living room carpet so softly that neither Stephanie or I had heard her.

I quickly tossed a sheet of paper towel over the ketchup-covered doll. But it was too late.

Mom winced. "How could you do that to Barbie?"

Stephanie scrambled up from her knees. "We were trying out special effects, Mrs. Dreyburgh. It's really awesome. You can stop the camera with Barbie's head on and then pop it off and start filming again. Want to see the movie so far?"

"No thank you. And put the ketchup away! Look at that. You've used up almost the whole bottle."

"Can we finish the video though, I mean after we put the ketchup away?" I asked.

Mom sighed and stared up at the ceiling, searching for the word No. "Why do you have to film in the living room anyway?" She was hedging, a very good sign.

"Nan's watching TV and the basement's too dark."

"And your room is too messy," Mom added.

I shrugged my shoulders. "We did spread a garbage bag on the rug."

"We'll clean it all up, Mrs. Dreyburgh. I'll wash the ketchup off Barbie. I'll even clean the garbage bag so you can use it again."

"You'll do that anyway."

"C'mon, Mom. Stephanie has a really cool idea for an explosion — "

"Hold on. You're not thinking of using real gunpowder . . . "

Stephanie and I shook our heads.

"Or firecrackers?"

We kept shaking our heads. We even raised our right hands, putting our left hands over our hearts in a kind of Girl Guide promise. We'd both dropped out of Brownies in grade three.

"No matches, not even gun caps?"

"No, honest, Mrs. Dreyburgh. We were just going to crumple up a white plastic bag and film it as it uncrumpled. We think it might look like smoke."

"All right. Fine. Nan wants to know if you're staying for supper, Stephanie."

"Sure. Um . . . if you don't mind."

"It's fine with me. Just don't put any ketchup on your steak or I'll be sick."

"Okay, Mrs. Dreyburgh."

So the horror picture turned into a sci-fi as we continued filming.

Barbie became an android — a cinch with mint jelly.

"It. Looks. Like. Green. Slime," Stephanie said, one word at a time to match the stop and start of the camcorder. I kept stopping the camcorder so that Stephanie could adjust Barbie's position or remove parts of her body.

The plastic bag as it uncrumpled looked surprisingly like a puffing smoke cloud although we decided we needed better sound effects for the explosions. Stephanie hissing "Poof, poof," just didn't cut it.

"Supper time," Nan called.

"And cut," I said as I stopped the camcorder.

"This could be our best picture yet," Stephanie raved as we walked toward the kitchen.

"I think so. And you know what else?"

"What?"

"The earrings must be working. I don't even feel hungry." We sat down at the table. My ear lobes still pulsed as though my heart had relocated there. I touched them and they felt hot.

"Are those new?" Patricia asked. A navy blue blazer hung over the back of her chair and she was wearing a crisp white shirt with the words GOLD-WALL SECURITY across the top of one pocket.

"Yeah, do you like them?" I twisted one of the backs, trying to get it to loosen its bite on my ear.

"They're different."

"Are button earrings a new fad?" Mom asked. "I can give you some of my old ones if you like."

"No, that's okay," I mumbled. "These are EZ-Slim earrings."

"What?" Mom asked.

"We bought them from The Shopping Network," Nan chimed in. "Supposed to help suppress your appetite."

"That doesn't sound healthy." Mom peered at my ears. "Do you think they're safe?"

"Yup, because they'll never work," Nan answered. "But the great thing is, everything from The Shopping Network's returnable. I sent back my arthritis anklets today."

"Why do you want to lose weight anyway, Lauren?" Patricia looked at me with a puzzled expression.

"Brenda told me Andrea lost ten pounds," Mom cut in. She sounded excited. "She's turned vegetarian apparently. First she cut off all the fat on her meat. Now she doesn't touch it at all."

I looked at the steak on my plate. Fat edged along the outside rim, springy and juicy with lots of steak spice and flavour. I took my knife and cut it off, pushing it to one side of the plate.

"Why don't you just exercise," Patricia suggested. "You could come to judo with me tonight."

"Nah, that's okay." Patricia had been taking judo for three years and was a blue belt. I was too wimpy. I'd probably just embarrass her. I cut off a tiny bite of steak and lifted it to my mouth.

"There's a mother-and-daughter tennis tournament coming up at the community centre, Lauren. You could take some lessons and we — "

"Thanks anyway, Mom." Sure sounded to me like they thought I should lose weight or they wouldn't be suggesting all this activity.

Mom stared at me for a few seconds. "Well, I don't like the idea of suppressing your appetite when you're a growing girl."

"Yeah, I'm growing all right," I mumbled, wondering whether I should leave the rest of my steak.

Stephanie tore into hers like some meat-eating dinosaur, then changed the topic. "If we don't use any more ketchup, do you mind if we film again tomorrow, Mrs. Dreyburgh? I have a sound tape and we thought we'd try out some better explosion sounds with our crumpled white bag effect."

"Just put the camcorder back in the case when you're done."

"Thanks, Mom."

I ate my salad with the same lite italian salad dressing Mom used. The earrings helped me resist my real favourite, the creamy ranch kind. I didn't have any brownies for dessert either.

After we drove Stephanie home I sat at my desk with a pad and pencil, trying to brainstorm ideas for my next presentation. Losing weight,

hmm . . . being fat . . . diets . . . low-fat recipes . . .
I wrote down anything that came to my mind. I
circled the groups of thoughts and tried to con-
nect them together. There didn't seem to be any
clear pattern.

And then the phone rang.

"Hi, Lauren?"

"Oh, hi Andrea."

"Um — do you really want to lose weight?" she
asked.

"Are you kidding? Of course. I'd do anything."
Then I thought for a moment. "Only I can't skip
breakfast . . . And I hate celery."

"None of that matters. You know Select Women,
Mom's gym?"

"Yeah."

"I've sort of joined. And I can bring a guest.
Wanna come?"

Something inside me wanted to say No so I
searched the ceiling. The word still wasn't there.
"When?"

"How about tomorrow after school?"

I took a deep breath. Still no reason not to. Not
with only a couple of months to the Halton Public
Speaking Competition. "Sure. Okay. What do I
need to bring?"

"Just something to do aerobics in — sneakers,
sweats or a leotard. We can walk from school."

"I'll bring my gym stuff tomorrow."

"See you then."

"Bye."

I went back to my presentation outline. A joke or an amazing statistic always made for a good jumping-off point. I could talk about my worst fear, turning into the piano-case lady. I could go through the various ways people try to lose weight. Maybe do some research as to what the success rate for each method was. I could finish with . . . What could I finish with? Maybe I could slip on a pair of Dad's pants and claim they were my "before" size. Maybe I could challenge the rest of the audience to shape up as well. I sighed. Twenty pounds would do it. If I lost twenty pounds I would have no problem giving a terrific speech. And if I lost ten pounds by the time I gave the in-class presentation in May, Jay would have noticed I was already on the way to becoming a knockout.

Someone tapped on my door. "Come in."

Patricia, still dressed in her judo *gi*, stepped into the room. "I'm having some cereal," she said. "You want some too?"

Patricia and I have been having these late night snacks off and on since we were little. I always like sitting with her, delaying bedtime by another fifteen minutes or so, eating breakfast food.

"None for me tonight, thanks." I twisted the gold buttons on my ears. "I'm stuffed."

"I think you're perfect the way you are, you

know," Patricia told me. The door closed softly behind her.

If it had been anyone else but Patricia who'd said it, I might have believed them. But what did Patricia know? She didn't have a boyfriend. And she needed to look bulky to frighten the shoplifters. Besides, she was my sister — she always stuck up for me.

I unscrewed my earrings to go to bed. While I brushed my teeth I glanced up in the mirror and noticed two pink spots marking my lobes where my EZ-Slims had been. I gently massaged them with my thumb and forefinger, but the pink wouldn't go away.

Next morning Nan's arthritis acted up. She cupped one hand around the other, her fingers slightly bent as though it would hurt too much to straighten them. "Do you mind fixing your own breakfast?" she asked. "There's eggs and bacon. The juice is in the fridge. Patricia made herself some french toast."

"That's okay, I'll just grab a Nutribar and eat it on the way to school."

"We don't have any Nutribars." Nan said. Then she looked me straight in the eyes. "You know, I saw a show on 'Oprah' the other day about teenage girls going on some really funny diets. Some kids really go overboard. Maybe I should order a copy of the show for you."

"That's okay, Nan, really. We watched a video on eating disorders in Health."

"Well, so you know all about it then, right?" Nan kept staring at me.

"Uh-huh."

"So let me just say this, Lauren. I bought you those earrings because they seemed like a harmless gimmick." Nan shook her finger at me now. "But don't let me catch you skipping any meals!" She watched me for an extra moment, trying to make me squirm. Finally she broke the silence. "Check in the cupboard. I think there's some Sugar Toasties or that Oats 'n' Bran cereal your mother always eats."

I grabbed my mother's cereal.

Nan pushed the brown sugar toward me. I shook my head. "Without anything," she said, "it'll taste about as good as those rice cookies you like so much."

"Rice *cakes*, Nan. Every meal doesn't have to have a million calories, you know."

"Yup, yup. I know. But did you know that only one out of two hundred and fifty dieters keeps the weight off over seven years? Then they all just gain it back and then some."

"Aw, Nan, do you believe everything Oprah says?"

"No, but it kind of makes you think, doesn't it?" Nan pushed up her purple frames with the back of her hand. "The makings for lunch are all out on the counter. Brownies, some chopped egg — I made that yesterday."

"Any leftover salad?"

"In the square Tupperware dish behind the mint jelly. You didn't have a sandwich in the living room yesterday, did you?"

"No, Nan. I know we're not allowed to eat in there."

"Hmm. I thought not. It's just that I found the jelly in the living room."

"Alien blood," I told her. "Mom won't let us use ketchup."

She rolled her eyes. "Now you just sit down with me and eat a bowl of cereal. Get the juice from the fridge."

The cereal did kind of remind me of the rice cakes. I looked toward the sugar bowl and then back at my flakes. How many calories would it take to make the cereal edible?

"You know, your mother often cuts a banana into that stuff. Adds some sweetness to it." Nan held a teacup between her open palms and sipped from it. "There's a banana on the counter."

I took Nan's suggestion. She also insisted I take an orange in my lunch along with my salad and the decoy brownie I had really packed for Stephanie.

"Oh, and Nan," I said as I headed out the door.

"Yes, Lauren?"

"I'll be late coming home from school. I'm going to work out at Select Women's Fitness Centre."

"Now Lauren, did you check with your mother on that?"

"Nah. But she won't mind. She wanted me to take tennis, remember? Just tell her I'm with Andrea." Andrea the vegetarian who's so good at losing weight.

I tucked my hair behind my ears as I reached down for my backpack.

"Lauren, your ears look all puffy and red. Maybe you should take those earrings off."

"No, no! No! Nan, could you just leave me alone? I have to get to school or I'll be late." With her around watching me all the time, how would I ever lose weight?

Nan kissed my cheek and as I headed away I shrugged my shoulder to wipe it off.

When I walked onto the school grounds I saw something that made my heart sink from my pulsing ear lobes down into my throat. Over by the fence, Kim was leaning back. Jay was leaning one arm against the fence, his hand close to Kim's cheek. If I were twenty pounds thinner, it could be *me* leaning back against that fence, the metal wires against *my* back, his hand near *my* face. Now he bent his face close to hers, and I could feel his breath warm against *my* face . . .

He was going to kiss her and I couldn't look

away. It was like watching it in slow motion. But Kim shoved him away with a backwards toss of her head, laughing. She looked like a model from a perfume ad.

"Hi, Lauren. I brought the sound-effects tape."

"Um — Oh hi, Stephanie."

"This is going to be so great." She shook the tape at me. "It's got the sound of chains rattling too. Maybe we could wrap some necklaces around Barbie and they'd look like . . . "

"Ohmygosh, Stephanie. I'm sorry, I forgot about filming after school. Can we do it tomorrow? Andrea asked me to exercise with her and . . . "

"You said yes?" Stephanie sounded shocked and maybe a little hurt.

"Well, she asked me, Steph. Look over there. Kim is stealing Jay from me faster than I can lose weight."

"Come off it, losing weight's got nothing to do with it. Besides, she'll get tired of him in a couple of weeks." Stephanie walked along beside me as we headed for our lockers. "I wonder why Andrea invited you along."

"What do you mean? Who else would she ask?"

"No one. Doesn't she usually only call you when she needs something?"

"C'mon Stephanie, that's a mean thing to say."

"Is it?" Stephanie didn't talk for a moment. Then she sighed. "It's okay about not filming today. Only tomorrow is basketball practice. It'll have to be Thursday."

"Thursday then. Don't sweat it." The bell rang then and we headed for home room.

At lunch time I gave Stephanie my brownie and found myself wondering how she could possibly put away so much food at one sitting. A sandwich, a pudding, an apple, my brownie and her tortilla chips lay spread around her. Then she bought herself a frozen yogurt from the cafeteria.

"Stop watching me," she said as she ate the yogurt. "I can't help it if I'm hungry." She jabbed her spoon toward Andrea. "Look at her, why don't you." She shovelled more yogurt into her mouth and spoke through it. "Andrea, you have two measly carrots and three celery sticks. Why do keep pushing them around? Can't you just eat them?"

Andrea covered her carrots and celery with her hands, like she was hiding a ketchupy Barbie. "I like to savour my food. If you wolf it down your stomach doesn't have a chance to register that it's full."

Stephanie rolled her eyes and huffed. "I'm enjoying my yogurt too, thank you very much."

It was strange, but for once in my life I sided with Andrea. Stephanie ate and ate and ate, almost inhaling the food. I tried to take my time eating my salad, leaf by leaf. I'd grabbed one of the vinegar packets from the cafeteria bin, the ones intended for the fries, and by the time I'd ripped the plastic open, Stephanie was already eating her pudding. I wasn't even finished peeling my orange when she polished off her chips. Then she spooned out the last bit of her yogurt as I chewed my last wedge of orange. She absorbed food, she ate so quickly, yet she was the thin one.

After school, I grabbed my things and followed Andrea out the door. She moved quickly ahead of me. Her elbows pumped behind her bouncing her backpack from side to side. Her hips wagged furiously in time with her backpack. I started breathing heavily as I rushed to keep up.

"Are we late?" I asked.

"No," Andrea puffed between strides, her face red and angry looking. "You want to lose weight, don't you? We're power walking. It burns more calories."

"Oh, okay." The backs of my calves began to burn. I didn't know if I'd have enough energy to work out after the walk.

At the studio, the woman behind the counter looked up from some paperwork and smiled. "Is this your first time with us at Select Women?"

"Um, yes," I said.

"Follow me then, please, and I'll give you the tour. My name's Cherry." She looked at Andrea. "You can come with us if you like." When Andrea hesitated I hooked my elbow into hers to drag her along.

Cherry wore a perky little baseball cap with SELECT WOMEN in hot pink letters, a white cotton knit shirt and shiny hot pink shorts. Her legs looked strong, with heavy muscles. "This is the whirlpool." She smiled patiently as we looked at the bubbly water. It smelled almost salty. I could imagine boiling spaghetti in it, but it was hard to picture a human lounging in the small pool, especially since it was empty now. "And over here, behind this door. . . " she pulled open the door and hot cedary smelling air blasted out " . . . is the sauna. Our tanning salon is near the entrance. Did you want to see it?"

I shrugged my shoulders.

"Follow me then." We walked over to the far end of the hall and she swung another door open. There in the centre of the tiny room, on a raised surface, lay a coffin-sized waffle iron with long white tube bulbs.

"Does it use any UV rays?" I asked.

"Um, not really harmful ones. Anyway, you don't have to use our tanning salon."

I could hardly believe it. People boiled, baked and grilled themselves at this place just to look good.

"Are you thinking of joining us?" Cherry asked as she took us to another room. THE CARDIO ROOM, the sign on the door read.

"Maybe," I said.

She smiled as she indicated the rows of machines. Four women walked on treadmills. One of them had on a Walkman, another read a book on a stand, the other two were browsing *Self* and *Fit* magazines. Three other women bicycled in the corner, a look of boredom glazing over their eyes and spreading onto their faces. A thin blond girl lay on a bench lifting a couple of barbells, snarling with each hoist.

"These are the showers," Cherry explained as we walked past some stalls. "And over here we have blow dryers for your convenience." A woman exercised her hair at the counter, aiming the blow dryer at it as she hung her head down and brushed the long strands vigorously. "The pool's on the top floor. Would you like to see it?"

I nodded.

"No," Andrea answered out loud. "Lauren wanted to try a class with me, and it's starting in two minutes."

"Fine. Before leaving you can come and check with me. That way Andrea can find out what she's won by bringing a guest to our club today."

Chapter 6

"Hup, hup, hup." The voice of the instructor boomed through the entire aerobics studio. *Boom, boom, boom!* The music hammered even louder, distorting her words. She adjusted a microphone that hung from a wire around her hot pink cap, and spoke in a low voice. "March it out, march it out, march it out."

Twenty of us marched it out in front of her. But the mirrors surrounding us made us seem like an army — an army wearing tights and exercise suits, halter tops, spandex shorts and leggings, sweat pants and T-shirts. I read some of their T-shirts as I marched with them. HALTON FIREHALL, JUST DO IT, ELVIS LIVE IN CONCERT. One woman had a big 81 across the back of her top. My mind tried to join all the words into some kind of sentence. *Halton Firehall Just Do It Elvis Live in Concert 81.* Not quite.

"Take it wide," the loud low voice commanded and a room full of women bent their knees and continued marching in a frog-like position. I became a frog too.

I watched the instructor for further commands.

She looked long and thin, more like a praying mantis than a frog.

Boom, boom, boom. "Grapevine," she growled and then shuffled to the left. The whole army miraculously shuffled with her, stopped when she did, clapped and hopped, and then shuffled to the other side.

I was so amazed that I shuffled, stopped, clapped and hopped a few counts late. Andrea bumped into me and then I bumped into ELVIS LIVE IN CONCERT, who had somehow shifted position till she was right beside me. A muffled giggle burst out of me, but Andrea and the Elvis lady ignored me. *Halton Firehall Just Do It 81,* I read now. Still not right.

The army shuffled on, clapping and hopping. After eight counts, I finally fell into step.

"March it out," Sergeant Praying Mantis bellowed. "Hup, hup, hup."

We took it wide, then swung our arms up. Andrea punched her arms high into the air till her face turned red with anger. It also turned damp. Some of the hair around her face shrivelled into moist tendrils.

"Grapevine," the praying mantis shouted. I was onto her now: Left. Clap, jump. Right. Clap, jump. Eight times.

March it out.

Take it wide.

Punch the air.

The formation ahead of me changed again. *Elvis Live in Concert Halton Firehall 81 Just Do It,* I read. No. It was hard to keep my brain focussed.

Light from the globes surrounding the mirrors shone off the army's skin. HALTON FIREHALL's neck glistened. Halter top's shoulders gleamed. I started noticing the other bizarre places where different women were sweating. The exercise suit ahead of me grew a wet tree-shaped patch in the middle of her back. Sergeant Praying Mantis moistened from the middle of her chest outwards. I raked my fingers through my hair. It had slunk down low and clung to my face in places. My face and neck felt feverish and soggy.

The sergeant cupped a hand to her ear. "Are we warm enough?" Somebody mumbled an answer.

"What's that?" she called louder.

"Yes," the army yelled back.

"March it out."

I watched the clock as we did all kinds of tricky shuffles, punches and lunges.

"Put some power into that thrust," Praying Mantis yelled.

What time was it? I looked over toward the clock in the far corner. The second hand floated around, the minute hand crawled. More marching, punching, kicking, hopping and sweating. After twenty minutes crawled by, we were supposed to find our pulse. My whole body boomed a rhythm.

"Keep moving!" Praying Mantis shouted. She marched and pressed a finger to her neck at the same time to show how it was done.

Everyone else in the room touched their neck too. It looked like some strange alien salute.

"There's a chart up there. Find your age and where your heartbeat's supposed to be."

My fingertips felt nothing at first, but when I found my pulse I counted as I marched to the *boom, boom, boom* of the music. I looked at the chart. Two red graph lines showed that my pulse should have been between twenty-five and thirty.

"Ten seconds is up, how'd we do?" the praying mantis asked.

I counted forty beats. Was I going to explode? Wait a minute, had I counted my heartbeats or my foot stomps? Or the *boom, boom*s in the music?

I looked over at Andrea. She was dripping now and her skin looked on fire. I could see her chest heaving in and out.

"Everybody where they should be?" our sergeant demanded. The army murmured yes noises. She didn't seem happy with this response. "Do we need to work harder?" she called out.

"No!" I yelled. ELVIS LIVE IN CONCERT gave me a backwards glance, her lip curled into a sneer. HALTON FIREHALL raised her eyebrows. Andrea shook her head.

The praying mantis just smiled, a creamy smooth, satisfied smile, the smile of someone in total power. "Grab a drink then. And we'll do three more sets."

JUST DO IT strolled to the water fountain. 81 picked up her water bottle and HALTON FIREHALL draped a towel around her shoulders. A strange thing happened. I looked around to see if anyone else would notice.

"Andrea, Andrea, read the backs of their T-shirts. Quick!"

Andrea mouthed the words. " 'Elvis Live in Concert eighty-one Firehall.' Yeah, so?"

"No! Eight-one, as in *ate* one. Get it?" She shook her head. "Ah, never mind." It was at that moment I missed Stephanie most.

After the cardio part of our workout, we did bizarre things with stretchy skipping ropes and our feet. We exercised our quads and triceps and then our abs — at least, that's what the sergeant said. And then we did cool-downs.

By then I was melting into a puddle. I grabbed a drink of water from the fountain and was about to head for the showers when I noticed Andrea on an exercise bike.

"You're going to do *more?*" I asked.

"Right now is peak fat-burning time," she answered, her feet a blur on the pedals.

"Huh?"

"The first twenty minutes you burn carbohydrates. Now it's all fat."

I thought for a moment, staring at my thighs. Was it possible? If I forced myself to cycle, could I melt off that weight today? I hoisted myself onto the hard triangular seat. It felt like a pointy rock. I pedalled once or twice, but my legs quivered and refused to pump.

"I'll be in the shower," I told Andrea as I climbed down from the rock. She was concentrating so hard she didn't notice.

Pool, I thought to myself as I grabbed my towel and headed for the stalls. Wouldn't it be great to relax in the pool? Why hadn't Andrea told me to bring a suit?

The shower stopped some of the quivering, but after I got dressed I sat like a vegetable on the bench by Andrea's locker. My EZ-Slims lay in my hand, but I was too tired to even move to the mirror.

"That looks like the beginning of an infection. I wouldn't put earrings on till that heals." Halton Firehall stood in front of me, only now without her T-shirt. Or anything else for that matter.

How could I talk to a person who was naked? I kept my eyes down while she rubbed a towel over various parts of her body.

"I have to put the earrings back on," I told her knees. "They help me lose weight."

"If you really want to lose weight, earrings aren't going to do it. Neither will this club." She gestured around, her large freckled hand sweeping under my nose.

"No?" I said as I counted the lint flecks on the carpet.

"No! It will help to firm and tone you, sure. But to lose weight, you need to change your whole lifestyle."

"Uh-huh," I glanced up to see whether she was dressed yet. Now she wore a different T-shirt: WEIGHT WHIPPERS the words across it read.

"You need to stop eating fat and eat more fibre. You have to exercise regularly. Have you ever been to a Weight Whippers meeting?"

"No. I thought that was only for — "

"Obese people? Not any more. If you want to lose ten pounds or more you can join."

I looked away as she slipped on some slacks. They were polyester like Nan's, only they had a zipper.

"Here, I have the schedule," she reached into her gym bag and handed me a sheet of paper. "If you want to come for a free meeting — I'm a leader at the two-thirty meetings on Wednesday, Thursday and Saturdays."

"Um, thanks." I tucked the paper into my pocket and waited till she left to get up and screw my EZ-Slims back on. My ear lobes pounded hard against the earrings, but I could honestly say at that moment I did not feel hungry.

Andrea dragged herself into the changeroom, pulled out her towel and headed for the showers. She looked even redder when she returned. "Do you think you'll join?" she asked.

"I'd never go alone, Andrea. Never. It's just too freaky."

"But you don't have to." Andrea glanced my way hopefully as she pulled on some baggy jeans. No block-shaped dresses for her any more. "I work out three times a week."

"We–ll, I don't know. I did get a card in the mail that lets me join for twelve dollars a month."

"That's great!" Andrea's voice bubbled up happily.

"But I only get twenty a month allowance. How could I live on just eight dollars?"

"My mother's paying for a basic membership for me." Andrea grinned. "Maybe she could talk to your mother."

"How much weight did you lose altogether?" I asked Andrea. Did I want to do this three times a week? I asked myself.

"Thirteen pounds in just under a month." Andrea raised her eyebrows at me.

Thirteen pounds would put me into the knock-out category for sure, and I still had all of April and some of May before the in-class presentation. I shrugged my shoulders. "Maybe."

"Come on. Let's go see Cherry now."

We walked back to the front desk. There, for the

first time, I noticed all the balloons stuck to the bulletin board along the wall. BRING A FRIEND AND WIN! the banner across the top read. Smaller signs around the balloons shouted *T-shirts! Water bottles! Cash prizes! Extended memberships!*

Cherry held a telephone receiver to her ear, snapping gum and chatting. When she saw us I heard her say, "Gotta go, bye." She smiled and stepped out from behind the counter with a thumb-tack in her hand. "All right, Andrea. Pick your balloon."

Andrea studied them for a second and then pointed to a purple one.

I covered my ears carefully so as not to press my EZ-Slims any tighter against my lobes. *POP!*

"Whoooo hoooooo!" Cherry shouted and applauded as she read the little note that fell out of the balloon. She handed Andrea a water bottle and applauded again. "Congratulations!" Then the phone rang and she picked up.

Andrea frowned at the bottle.

"What's wrong?" I asked. "You don't like their T-shirts anyways."

"I wanted to upgrade my membership."

"What?"

"I want to be able to come every day of the week. Mom says we have gym at school. That three times is plenty."

I frowned at her now. "Seven times a week!" I

repeated. "Are you crazy, Andrea!"

Cherry hung up the phone. "So, Lauren, did you want to join? If you do — both you and Andrea get to choose a balloon."

I squeezed my eyes shut. "I have to ask my mom," I told her.

"Sure. Listen, here's the form, and here's my card. And my name is . . . " she pointed to her name tag.

"Cherry." I smiled at her.

"And if you want to come back, the rest of this week is free. Andrea can pick another balloon each time."

Andrea brightened at this. We waved and left.

"I sure would like to win an extended membership," Andrea hinted as we stepped onto the sidewalk.

"Why do you want to work out all the time?"

"Because it's like a war I have to fight." Andrea's hands bunched into fists. She was walking slower now than we had on the way to Select Women. "My body wants to be fat just like my dad's. And no matter how little I eat, my body makes it into fat." Now she sped up into her power march. "Don't you see, Lauren, I *have* to exercise every day to win that war!"

I stared at Andrea as we sped along. She faced forward, not even glancing my way. Her blue eyes no longer seemed doll-like. They focussed straight ahead like an eagle's, hard and determined. They didn't seem to see things to the left or the right. Everything in her seemed aimed toward one goal, losing weight.

I felt a bit envious and a little in awe of her. She sure had willpower once she made her mind up. And at that moment, even though I understood exactly what she meant, I felt nervous, too. Just how far would Andrea go?

Chapter 7

"Please, please come to Select Women with me again." We were at the end of the walkway to my house. I turned to go but Andrea grabbed onto my jacket sleeve. "You helped with my speech — I know I can help you lose weight."

"What if I'm too sore?" I knew I didn't want to go back to Select Women even while it was free. It was too boring.

"You won't be. I wasn't. C'mon, Lauren."

"Maybe we'll have a lot of homework. I don't know what Mom has planned." Nothing could make Andrea release my sleeve. "I'll let you know tomorrow, okay?" Finally she let go. "Bye." I waved.

Down the walk, through the door, up the stairs to my room I trudged, every muscle heavy and soggy like a wet sponge. Finally I flopped across my bed. "I'm home, Nan," I shouted. But my words were muffled by my pillow and Nan didn't answer. Strange. She should have been expecting me by now, listening for me. I felt a little disappointed, maybe even a little annoyed with her. Hmpf! Oh well, at least I could just lie there on my bed, my toughest exercise to breathe deeply.

Someone knocked at my door.

"Lauren," my mother's voice called from the other side. "Supper time."

I touched my burning ear lobes. I didn't feel very hungry. Maybe I could try skipping one meal. Then I wouldn't have to budge. "I ate something at Andrea's, Mom."

Mom pushed through the door. "Come down anyway and share your company with us."

"Oh all right." I peeled myself from the bed and slunk after her.

"Oh, and Lauren," she turned to me at the bottom of the stairs.

"Yeah?"

"Nan's arthritis is still acting up. Do you think you could vacuum the family room after supper?"

"Aw Mom, can't it wait till Nan's feeling better?"

"No. I don't want her straining herself to do it."

"Then can't Patricia? I'm beat. I went to aerobics with Andrea."

Mom's eyelids flickered. "Patricia was on her feet all day, and I showed ten houses to the Morrisons. They dragged along their pre-schoolers too." She pushed me gently toward the kitchen. "Don't make a fuss," she hissed.

Patricia passed me the casserole dish as I slid into my chair. Shepherd's pie. Mmm, it smelled wonderful. Even though I really wasn't hungry I took a couple of large spoonfuls. "Would you pass the milk, please, " I asked Nan.

"Sorry, I didn't get over to the store today. We're all out."

"Here's the water. It's good for our complexion anyway," Mom said as she put her filter water container on the table.

I poured myself a glass. I would have loved some milk to go with the mashed potato crust of Mom's pie. Why couldn't Nan have bought some, or asked Mom to? I touched my EZ-Slims, licked my lips and sipped at the water.

"Remember what we discussed," Mom told me pointedly as she loaded the supper plates into the dishwasher.

"Yeah, sure."

Our vacuum cleaner weighs eight hundred pounds, and sometimes the power head works. Tonight it didn't, so I aimed the nozzle at lint flecks all over the carpet, making little circles.

"Is the Ty–D–Bol under the bathroom sink?" Patricia asked, carrying a pail down the hall.

"Yup," I heard Nan answer. I decided not to complain about the vacuum cleaner. I hate cleaning toilets even more than vacuuming. I manoeuvred the nozzle over some more flecks and made a new batch of circles. If Mom heard the roar of the vacuum long enough, I was hoping she'd let me off soon.

She came into the room then, her hands on her hips. "You missed over there. Wait a minute. I'll move the couch and you can reach under." She pushed the sofa to one side and then back. "There. Now under the coffee table. Uh-huh. Along the baseboards. Did you already flip the cushions on the sofa?" She made me vacuum the curtains, and even the corners of the ceilings.

Stupid arthritis, hope Nan gets better fast, I thought as I flung myself back down on my bed an hour later. "I'm never going to move again," I promised the ceiling, and didn't till the next morning.

When the alarm rang I headed for the bathroom, and as usual stepped onto the scale. I'd lost seven pounds! "Yyess, yyess!" I grinned at myself in the mirror. I danced back to my room after brushing my teeth and grabbed my tightest jeans from the closet. Pulling the zipper up was still rough, but I lay on the bed to do it. I slipped on my brightest red T-shirt — the one I save for special days — and even found my lucky red socks. I screwed on the EZ-Slims and danced down the stairs.

I expected to have to argue with Nan about not eating one of her huge syrupy breakfasts, but her hands still ached so she hadn't made anything.

"There are some strawberries in the fridge," she told me.

The strawberries sweetened the Oats 'n' Bran

just perfectly and there were some left to pack in my lunch. Terrific. My ear lobes were pounding, but maybe that's the way the EZ-Slims worked. I felt light and skinny and beautiful.

The phone rang and I knew who it would be. As I picked up the receiver I also knew what I had to say. "Hi, Andrea. Sure I'll come." EZ-Slims or Select Women or maybe both, who knows? I wasn't ready to stop using either.

"Stephanie, does it show?" I called the moment I saw her near the school gate.

"What, what?"

"I lost seven pounds." I smiled at her, sucking in my shrinking tummy even further to show off the weight loss.

"Gee, hmm," she looked me up and down, her eyebrows bunching. "You do look nice."

"Thank you." Maybe when you're with someone a lot it's hard for them to notice. Or maybe Steph felt a titch jealous — her fat friend becoming knock-out material. I was too excited to get annoyed with her just then. "I just can't believe it, in one day!"

"Really? I didn't think you could lose that much in one day."

Now I *was* starting to get annoyed with her. "Well, maybe it was over a few days and the scale just suddenly showed it. You know, all the used-up calories suddenly added up and then subtracted." I threw up my hands. "I don't know."

Stephanie shook her head.

I wanted to shake her. "The scale doesn't lie. Anyway why do you have to be so negative?"

She opened her mouth to say something but we didn't even get a chance to argue.

"Hi, Lauren."

It was my lucky day. I turned in time to see Jay's cool grey eyes giving me a quick up and down.

"Hi, Jay."

He pointed his finger at me. "Something different about you today."

I felt my face warming. "Thanks."

He nodded for a few seconds. "Have you been to the new Economart yet?" he finally asked.

"Nah, I don't like shopping there."

"Me neither." He smiled. "But they have great CDs, almost as many as Rocketman's. You have to go there."

"Maybe I will sometime."

"Yeah, yeah." Jay concentrated now on something, or rather someone, in the distance. "Maybe I'll see you there." He loped off to catch up to Kim.

"Wow, he practically asked you on a date," Stephanie said.

I grinned. "See! Some people notice my amazing weight loss."

"Weight *schmeight*. You should have offered to go with him."

"Oh, I don't know . . . "

"Think about it. Ask yourself what Kim would do."

We drifted into English class. Hmm, what *would* Kim have done? I pictured myself standing with my hand above a pushed-out hip. *"Why don't we go together after school, Jay?"* Only in that picture I saw Kim's body attached to my head, and Kim's hair growing from it — as though if I lost weight I expected to become Kim. I daydreamed my way through the morning. Ms Smyrnios didn't catch me.

At lunch time, still in that dreamy mood, I watched as Stephanie and Andrea sat down beside me. A kaiser bun, an apple, three cookies, a bag of mini crackers with cheese — Stephanie piled it all up in front of her and then joined the cafeteria line-up.

Andrea took a knife from her backpack along with her container of vegetables. Only one stick of celery today and one carrot. She began cutting them up. It was a painstaking operation and she frowned with concentration. Then she arranged the carrot and celery slices in rows, nibbled at one and rearranged them all, this time in an alternating pattern.

Why did she keep pushing them around so much? I wondered as I took out my own sandwich and dessert and Stephanie sat down with a large plate of fries and gravy.

Ah, my dessert — strawberries. I smiled at

them. They were nutritious yet somehow sweet and enticing. Hordes of cafeteria kids would down gooey chocolate desserts, but I held my head high, chewing smugly. I would not succumb. Then I noticed Andrea studying my sandwich. Her forehead was all wrinkled. "Something wrong?"

"Is that bologna?" she asked, frowning so hard her eyes almost squeezed shut.

"So whaa? Whaa's it oo yoo?" Stephanie said, her mouth full of fries.

"Lauren wants to lose weight. I'm only trying to help," Andrea answered.

"It's bologna," I said softly. "Is that okay?"

"Do you have mayo or cheese on it?" she asked, peeling off the top slice of bread. She clicked her tongue at the round pink slice.

"No, just mustard."

"That's good. You can eat the bread then, but the bologna is full of fat."

"Oh give me a break," Stephanie sputtered as I pulled it off my bread.

"You eat it then!" Andrea challenged.

Steph snatched up the bologna. "Watch me." She rolled it up, dipped it into her gravy and stuffed the whole slice into her mouth.

Andrea gasped and then stood up. "You'll excuse me," she said, scooping her line-up of vegetables back into her container. "I just remembered something I need from my locker." She stuck the container into her backpack, heaved it up on one shoulder. "See you after school, Lauren," she said, and walked away.

Stephanie licked her fingers. "What does she mean? You're not going to Select Women again?" she asked as I ate my mustard-and-bread sandwich.

"You have basketball practice anyway."

"Yeah, but I thought maybe you'd work on your presentation in the library. Then when I was done practice you could come home with me for supper. Dad's making lasagna."

"Aw, I can't, Steph. Not just because of the aerobics class. I'm really dieting this time."

"Fine, fine." She started tearing into her kaiser bun.

"Please, Steph, it's really working!"

"I said it was fine."

But she didn't mean it. She ploughed through her entire lunch as I went through my dessert, berry by berry, two nibbles each. "Why don't we both go and work on our presentations now," I suggested.

"I don't even know my topic," she grumbled.

"Ms Smyrnios said to do anything that interests you, which means you have only one choice." We both grinned. "Let's go check what the resource centre has on weight loss . . . aaannd horror movies!"

The library technician wasn't around so I raced Stephanie to the new computer. An encyclopedia page was already displayed on the screen. "Me first," I said. I keyed in "Dieting" and clicked on SEARCH. "Hmm, what I need is something to open with." Steph peered over my shoulder.

This neat-looking diagram of a machine came up along with some information about die forging. "Not quite." I shook my head.

"I know, try 'Obesity,' " Stephanie suggested.

I nodded my head and typed in the letters. This time when I hit SEARCH, *Oberammergau, The Passion Play in 1984* came up, with an even better colour picture of some guys in robes.

"Awesome, eh?" Stephanie said. We both stared at it for a couple of seconds. "Maybe I'll just go look in the regular encyclopedias."

"Aw, aren't you going to help me?" I complained to her back as she walked away.

"What are you having trouble with?" a voice said from behind me.

"Obesity."

"Oh, I think you're looking pretty good lately," Jay quipped.

"I — uh — I mean, I need some information on obesity for my speech," I whispered. Our second meeting today. I felt a smile start from the bottom of my toes and reach through my body right up to my ears.

"Piece of cake." Jay shrugged. "You're set for pictures instead of articles. He dragged the mouse and clicked a couple of times. "There you go."

"Thanks, " I breathed at him softly.

He winked. "No prob," he said and strolled toward the new book display. I loved that walk of his. He didn't bob or saunter like other guys. His long legs took confident smooth strides.

I continued watching him as he picked up a manual on the Internet: *Wired World*. I even loved his hands. They easily palmed that huge book as he thumbed through it. No chewed or dirty nails either. I watched as he walked past the technician's desk.

"Hey, you forgot to check the manual out," I called, but the words came out weak and a little hoarse, so he didn't hear me. Oh well.

"All right!" Stephanie gushed as she zoomed over with an open yellow book in her hand. "He asked you to the mall didn't he?"

"No." I gestured toward the screen. "He helped me with the search."

"Great. And check this out." She shoved the book at me.

"What is it?"

"*The Guinness Book of Records.* Look." Stephanie flipped back to the first page. At the top it read "Human Being."

"Eeeew, what happened to him?" I stared down

at some sort of tribal person who had a dish stuck in his mouth.

"Her. The women in the Surma tribe wear this. It's a ceremonial lip plate."

"Looks painful," I said, taking the book from her and staring at the picture more closely. "Hey, wait a minute." I flipped through the pages past the stuff on giants and midgets. "Here it is, Steph." I stopped at the weight section. "I've just come up with the perfect opening."

Chapter 8

Later that afternoon I survived my second aerobics class at Select Women, another cause to celebrate. On our way out Andrea picked her second balloon. This time the little paper inside said she'd won a free T-shirt.

"Yuck. I hate it," she whispered to me as she held it up by the shoulders. "It's so . . . vulgar."

"I don't know." I looked at it from an angle, remembering the pink lettering stretched across Andrea's chest the day she wore her mother's T-shirt. And I remembered what Jay had said: "Andrea's hot!"

"You want it?" she asked, holding it out to me.

"Sure." I took it by the shoulders.

"It's yours then." Andrea smiled as I started folding. "Are you coming back tomorrow?"

Too late I saw the trap. I stopped folding.

"I won't bug you after that," she promised. "If you join or not, it's up to you. But I could still win the extended membership . . . "

There was a bit of the old Andrea left in that pleading doll-eyed look. It made me feel more relaxed than the new eagle-eyed weight losing machine she'd become. I folded the T-shirt two more times and tucked it in my backpack. "Okay. One more day won't hurt, I guess."

"Great. Thanks!"

We power walked out of the gym into the cool moist air. My left ear lobe felt a bit itchy and I reached up to twist the EZ-Slim around. I felt a wetness there — sweat or maybe water left over from my shower. It wasn't raining, was it? I looked up at the grey April sky. No, no rain.

"See you tomorrow," I told Andrea when we reached my house. I felt energetic enough to spring up the walk and bounce into the house. Knowing that I'd lost seven pounds had given me a happy lightness the whole day.

"Nan, hi, I'm home!" I called as I hung up my jacket. She didn't come to the hall like she usually did. "Nan! Na-aaaa-n!" I hollered. No response. I drifted out to the kitchen to look for her.

"Hi, Lauren. Do you feel like pizza or fried chicken for supper tonight?" Patricia stood at the counter, the yellow pages in front of her, a phone in her hand.

"Where's Nan?" I asked, feeling annoyed and a little worried too.

"Mom took her to Dr. Worden to see about the arthritis. Hey, what happened to your ear? There's blood dripping from it!"

"Huh?" I touched my ear. "It's nothing. I guess my earrings are a little tight."

"You better take them off," Patricia said. "Did you know you have a big rip in your shirt?"

"Where? Where?"

"Under your arm. Pizza or chicken?"

"Pizza." My fingers touched skin. I moved them along the tear and realized my whole armpit must have been on display every time I had reached for something. How long had I been walking around like that? In the resource centre, when I was talking to Jay? Oh gees . . . "I'm going to go change."

"Pepperoni or vegetarian?" she called after me.

"I don't care." All my energy and lightness had leaked out of that armpit hole. But seven pounds is still seven pounds, I told myself, heading for the bathroom to admire my new lower weight.

The dial swung around and rested by the red line. "What! That can't be right." I jiggled my feet. The dial shifted back and forth but then came to rest at the same number. I quickly emptied my jean pockets and stepped back on. Same weight. I tore off my socks and shoes and tried again.

My jeans must be very heavy, I decided. I stripped down to my underwear and got back on the scale. The dial swung around and I found out my clothes weighed two pounds. But that didn't matter, I realized, because this morning I had worn exactly the same stuff when I'd weighed myself.

The only thing that mattered was that I'd gained back the whole seven pounds I'd lost.

I slipped back into my jeans and started breathing fast and hard as I stared in the mirror. *Fat, fat, fat.* A drop of blood slid down from behind my left EZ-Slim. I unscrewed the backs of both earrings and touched wet little crusts. Ugh. I rinsed off my ear lobes and the water ran down red into the sink. I dabbed on disinfectant that stung like crazy.

Disgusted, I sat down on the closed toilet lid, bloody EZ-Slim in my hand. *Fat, fat, fat,* even though I'd worked out two days in a row, power walked home, eaten Oats 'n' Bran for breakfast. I'd even given my bologna to Stephanie and I couldn't remember my last dessert. And what did I have to show for it? Two scabby ears. My eyes burned with angry tears.

"What's the matter?" Patricia head peeked in around the door. "Do they hurt that much?"

"No!" I moaned. "It's just that I'm working so hard to lose weight and this morning when I weighed myself I'd lost seven pounds." I ripped off some toilet paper from the roll hanging there. "Now I check again and I've gained it all back."

"Oh." Patricia came in and sat down on the edge of the tub, frowning.

"Is that all you're going to say? 'Oh?' " I wiped my eyes and blew my nose.

"No. I guess not." She leaned forward, planting

her elbows on her thighs. She propped her chin up with her hands. "It's my fault."

"Oh, c'mon Patricia, how can that be?" I slipped the used toilet paper into the wastepaper basket.

"Well, when I washed the bathroom floor last night, I had to move the scale around ... "

"Yeah, but it's in exactly the same place as it always is."

"Uh-huh, only I must have accidentally moved the little adjusting wheel at the back."

"So?"

"Just before, when I went to the bathroom, I noticed a spider crawling across the scale. And the dial showed that it weighed seven pounds less than zero. I knew spiders were light but how could that be? That's when it hit me that I must have moved the little adjusting wheel when I washed the floor. And so I pushed it back again." Patricia winced as she finished explaining. But the doorbell rang then, saving her. "That must be the pizza. I better go get it."

She disappeared. I closed my hand tightly around the earrings. Everything had gone so well when I'd lost the seven pounds. *Thought* I'd lost the seven pounds, I corrected myself. I stood up and stared into the mirror. I wanted to wing the EZ-Slims at my reflection. *Fat, fat, fat.* I couldn't stay this way no matter what. I took a deep breath. "All right," I said as I stood up. "All right!" I repeated loudly at my face. "So what are you going to do about it?"

"Come and get it while it's hot!" Patricia called.

I stomped down the stairs. Even though my stomach growled at the spicy tomato smell, I took one slice of pizza. Only one. And then I nibbled.

When Mom and Nan finally joined us I still had a piece of crust left.

"Take some more pizza, Lauren, I ordered plenty," Patricia said. Then she turned to Nan. "What did the doctor say."

"Oh, nothing much. Asked me if I wanted to try gold injections."

"Gold injections?" I repeated. It sounded like another Shopping Network solution to me.

"Yup, apparently the gold gives amazing results."

"Sometimes!" Mom corrected. "Other times patients have bad reactions and end up in wheelchairs."

Nan shrugged her shoulders. Then she lifted a slice of pizza from the box onto her plate. "Could you get me some water, Lauren?"

"Sure," I grumbled. I wanted Nan back to normal, serving me. My stomach still growled for more pizza.

I placed the glass in front of her and she unscrewed a little pill bottle. "Anyway, he did give me a different prescription to try." She popped a capsule in her mouth and sipped at her water, swallowing the capsule.

"Speaking of bad reactions," Mom said, "look at Lauren's ears. They're all scabby!"

"Is that what those earrings did?" Nan asked me.

I nodded quickly.

"Well, we'll ship 'em back, Lauren, honey. Don't you worry about that."

I glanced down at my last bit of pizza. It was looking really good. "But the EZ-Slims worked. I wasn't hungry all the time."

"Aw, Lauren, it was all in your mind. The earrings were just a gimmick," Nan said.

"And anyway, I don't care if they worked," Mom insisted. "I won't have you scarring yourself like that for any reason, Lauren. I don't like all this dieting nonsense. If you ask me, you're walking a thin line."

"Say, I've got an idea," Nan interrupted.

I picked up my crust and then put it back down.

"When I'm feeling better, you can go line dancing with me."

I groaned. Judo, tennis, line dancing — Andrea's aerobics class was looking better and better.

Stephanie stacked her lunch on the table: two sandwiches, an apple, a bag of chips, a pudding cup and three cookies. "You're going to Select Women again!" she said as she chomped into the sandwich. "But I brought the sound effects tape. You promised we'd film today."

"I never *promised*, Stephanie. Besides, I only have a couple more free days." I watched her start into her lunch. "You're not going to eat all that, are you?"

"Yes I am!" she huffed at me, packing up her lunch again. "But not here!" She walked over to the other end of the cafeteria and sat with the girls on her basketball team.

"What's wrong with her?" Andrea asked as she slid into the seat across from me. I explained about the filming. "Well, you know if you join the gym, Stephanie could always come as your guest. And anyway, right now when you're dieting, she's not the best person to have around."

That's not true! I wanted to say, but then I looked over to where Stephanie now sat, scoffing chips and a pudding cup at the same time. She waved around her chip bag, offering some to the team. I remembered the chocolate cupcakes with white icing squiggles that she always brought me, and sighed. "I guess you're right."

So that was lunch, but the whole day went just as badly. Jay didn't wink, smile or even look my way, even though I'd worn my new Select Women T-shirt, the one he'd liked so much on Andrea.

I told Andrea about sending back the EZ-Slims, and my disappointment about the scale on the way to the Select Women Fitness Centre. Huff, puff, huff, puff.

"You don't need those earrings. And from now on, you should only weigh yourself on the Select Women scale. It's always right." She spoke as though I were definitely joining, and surprisingly, I didn't correct her.

After we changed Andrea showed me where the scale was, and got on. "I've lost another two pounds. Your turn." She smiled.

"Wow, Andrea, so fast? That's amazing!" I stepped on then . . . and realized that now Andrea weighed three pounds less than I did.

I put angry power behind every move as we march-shuffle-hop-lunge-punched our way through another one of Praying Mantis's classes. I pumped at the stationary bicycle after the class too, and when I saw Halton Firehall near the shower, I told her I was planning to attend one of her Weight Whippers meetings. It might be the one edge I could gain over Andrea.

"Well, here's my card," she said. "Why don't you come this Saturday? The meeting starts at two-thirty."

Usually I hung around with Steph, but seeing as she wouldn't even eat with me, this Saturday would be different. "Thanks, I'll see you there."

I stepped away quickly when Andrea came back from the showers.

On the way out again, she got to pick another balloon.

"Congratulations!" Cherry slapped her back and shook her hand. "You've won the extended membership."

At least it was someone's lucky day.

Chapter 9

I didn't tell anyone where I was going. Mom and Nan figured I was heading over to Steph's, but she had a basketball tournament and wasn't talking to me anyway. And Andrea didn't expect me to hang around with her. Between her horse-riding lessons and her Saturday workout, she probably didn't have time. I'd straighten everyone out when I was sure this was what I wanted to do.

I wore my dark sunglasses and a baseball cap, hoping not to be noticed as I ducked into the Weight Whippers office. Maybe the fact that it was a cold grey Saturday made me stand out just a little.

"Can I help you?" the receptionist asked, looking at me over her owl glasses.

"No. I'm just visiting." I showed her Halton Firehall's card.

"Oh yes, Kate Luzinsky, she's one of our weight-loss leaders."

"Uh-huh. She told me I could attend a Weight Whippers meeting. I met her at Select Women."

"That's fine. You don't have to weigh in then.

Just step around to the meeting room."

That's when I first noticed the other women lined up in front of two booths. Some of them were taking off sweaters, glasses, watches.

I walked around the line-ups and found myself a metal folding chair in the back. In the front, a television set played a video of women talking about the effect their weight loss had had on their lives. To the side, two piano-case ladies, overflowing in their chairs, snapped into some celery as they spoke about a recipe.

"The pumpkin counts as a vegetable so you can eat as much as you like."

"But Synthisweet tastes so bitter."

"Oh no. You cook the pumpkin first. Then you add the Synthisweet. It tastes just like pumpkin pie — without the crust of course."

Sugar Crisp without the sugar, corn flakes without the corn and saltines without the salt. I smiled, thinking about what Stephanie had said about the rice cakes that day when we first tasted them. One by one, the women trickled in from the weigh-in booths.

"I only lost half a pound," a lady Nan's age told another older woman as they chose their chairs. "But I was bad, Doris. So bad. You know that cheesecake that Desserts Unlimited serves?"

"The one with the mocha swirl through the middle and the shortbread crust?"

"That's the one." The woman shook her head and frowned. "I was just going to taste a bite of Lorne's, but then it was so rich and creamy."

Doris nodded sympathetically. "Their cheesecake is the best, isn't it, Charlene?"

"You know it," she groaned. "And before I realized what I was doing I'd eaten the whole piece."

Doris shook her head now too. They both looked sad.

The rows of metal chairs filled with women placing their glasses back on their faces, strapping their watches to their wrists, slipping on shoes.

Halton Firehall stepped up to the front. "Hello everyone. I'm Kate Luzinsky. I lost seventy-eight pounds through Weight Whippers and I'm here to show you how."

The rows of seated women clapped and smiled.

"Who here has lost ten pounds?" Halton Firehall looked around expectantly.

Three women raised their hands. The applause became louder. Kate walked over and handed each of the women a happy-face bookmark.

"And who here has exercised at least three times this week?"

More hands shot up. More applause. Kate strolled up and down the rows handing out . . . I wasn't sure what she was handing out till she stopped near me. "You've exercised three times this week. I know it because I saw you at Select

Women." She ripped off a little piece of white paper from a narrow roll and handed it to me. On it were three aerobic-people stickers. Where would I stick them? I wondered as I rubbed my finger over the fuzzy blue figures. I felt rewarded somehow. If I joined Select Women I could collect lots of aerobic-people stickers.

I looked over at Charlene and calculated. She lost half a pound a week sneaking cheesecake. Since I wanted to lose twenty pounds, that would take me, oh, about forty weeks, which would give me a hundred and twenty fuzzy-blue-people stickers. Not bad.

But wait a minute. I needed to lose the weight by the public speaking competition which was in June, a couple of months or — again I calculated — eight weeks away. Half a pound a week just wouldn't do it.

Now there was more wild applause as a slim young woman stood up and stepped to the front to accept her lifetime membership into Weight Whippers.

"Do you have to join for life?" I asked the woman beside me.

"Well, it is a lifelong battle."

The young woman had lost twenty pounds in four months.

I felt panicky. How would I do it in time?

Next Kate asked if anyone had any difficult

moments to share with the group, and Charlene, the cheesecake lady, raised her hand.

Kate motioned to her and Charlene told everyone how it had been her sixty-ninth birthday and she had just wanted a taste of cheesecake and blah, blah, blah.

"Aw that's too bad," one of the piano-case ladies murmured.

"Don't worry about it, honey," the other one said.

Kate listened, her hand supporting her cheek, her mouth turned slightly upward at the corners. "Never mind. You did well," Kate said when Charlene finished speaking. "You had a minor setback but then you went straight back to your new healthier life plan." She started clapping and everyone joined in. Somebody started singing "Happy Birthday" and suddenly the whole room was singing along, even me.

Charlene's eyes turned shiny and at the end she thanked us all. "I feel so comfortable with this group, I'm going to share something with you that I've never told anyone before. When I was sixty-three my hair started falling out for no reason, and by the time I was sixty-five — " she gripped the top of her head now and pulled off her hair " — I was as bald as a turkey."

A hush fell over the room. I stared at her. And she was worried about a piece of cheesecake? Suddenly applause thundered from the rows of women.

Stephanie would have got a real kick out of this bunch. Still, what choice did I have? The rice cakes didn't work, and the EZ-Slims wrecked my ears. It was time for something drastic. Next Kate lectured with a flip chart and a pointer about fats. She talked about cholesterol and saturated and unsaturated fat. About animal versus vegetable fats. It was amazing. It was frightening. I sat up a little straighter. How can people eat so much fat? I would never touch any again, ever. A while later the meeting was over and everyone applauded again.

"Any new members please stay behind so that I can take a moment to explain the program." She looked at me. "You too, Lauren."

I moved to the front with the other new members. Kate handed me a pamphlet with seven days worth of rectangles labelled Breakfast, Lunch, Supper and Snack. At the bottom of each page were circles labelled Fat, Protein, Dairy, Vegetable, Fruit and Carbohydrate.

"Everything you eat should be entered in your food diary," she explained to us. "Then you colour in the circle of the food group. The number of circles represents how many servings you're allowed. Of course, you can have as many vegetables as you want."

"Of course," one of the other ladies agreed.

"You must drink eight to ten glasses of water a day. Try to get as much fibre as you can." Now Kate took out a little binder full of handouts. "You'll get these when you join, Lauren. The rest of you make sure you read them. See you next week."

"What do I need to do to join?" I asked.

"Twenty dollars for registration and twelve dollars a week, plus a letter from a parent or guardian giving you permission."

"Well, maybe I'll see you around," I said. Thirty-two dollars the first meeting? That was nearly my entire EZ-Slim money. And permission from Mom? Forget it. She was already on my case about my dieting. But as I left I saw a framed photo standing on the table at the front. On one side the Kate I knew was wearing a firehat, a heavy rubber coat and tall black boots. On the other side was the piano-case lady.

"Before and After," she told me. "I owe my job to Weight Whippers. Without them I could have never passed the physical."

You couldn't put a price on something like that, I decided. I'd have to hit Nan up for the money.

As soon as I got home I dashed to the kitchen sink. Eight glasses of water! I thought I'd drink them all and get it over with.

"That you, Lauren?" Nan called.

The first glass was easy.

"Goodness, you must be thirsty," Nan said as she came into the kitchen. "You couldn't wait to take off your coat?"

I shook my head as I started on the second glass. I needed to stop halfway through and take a breath.

"There's some chocolate milk in the fridge. Patricia bought groceries on her lunch hour."

"No thanks," I said. I managed to down the third glass, but began to feel like I was turning into a fish tank. "Nan," I gasped between gulps, "I need to borrow some money from you. It's really important."

"You know you can always come to Nanna when you're in trouble. What do you want, five dollars till next allowance?"

In my mind I calculated: to join Select Women it would cost a hundred and forty-four for the year. To join Weight Whippers I'd need twelve dollars a week for the six weeks that were left before the speech competition, plus twenty bucks for registration. That made ninety-two. "Nan, I have to have two hundred thirty-six dollars."

"What!"

"Well, some of it I can pay back with my EZ-Slim money."

"The earrings are still on my credit card. You never paid for those. Why do you need all this money, Lauren?"

I explained about the health club fees, and as Nan's mouth twisted into a frown, I told her about Weight Whippers.

"Lauren, I can't just say yes to all this. We have to talk to your mom."

"C'mon, Nan, I'm in trouble. I'm fat and I want to join Select Women and Weight Whippers. I have to!"

Nan's mouth twisted even more. "You are *not* fat, you're just big-boned like me."

"You said you were skinny at my age!"

"At your age?" Nan pursed her lips as she thought. "Well, yes. Exactly like you."

"You said as skinny as a broomstick." I squeezed my eyes into a hard thin stare.

"Don't look at me like that. I'm an old woman. I can't be expected to remember all these details."

Now I clicked my tongue and rolled my eyes.

"Besides, in my day they would have thought you were skinny as a broomstick." Nan shook her head. "Listen, Lauren. A lot of people join clubs and then after a while, drop out. That's how the clubs make their money."

"Not me, Nan. I'll go to Select Women three afternoons a week, and I'll go to a Weight Whippers meeting every week. I promise. Please!"

"You're really determined, aren't you?"

I gulped more water and nodded frantically.

"Well . . . I'm sorry, Lauren, we still have to talk with your mom."

Augh! Nan could be so frustrating I wanted to scream at her. But if I did I'd probably gurgle. The fish tank pressed so hard against my bladder I stomped off to the bathroom instead.

And then at supper I had to repeat the whole

discussion with Mom, along with three more glasses of water and a couple of bathroom breaks.

"All right, Lauren," Mom finally said. "You say you're serious about the fitness club. I figure exercise can't hurt you. So here's the deal. I'll pay for your registration at Select Women *if* you vacuum the family room every Friday after school and clean the bathroom twice a week."

"Not the toilet, please. Anything but the toilet," I pleaded, pressing my hands together, prayer style.

"Of course the toilet bowl, it's part of the bathroom, isn't it?"

How serious was I really? She watched me as I thought it over. Serious enough to march, shuffle and lunge with the spandex army three times a week? Serious enough to write down every morsel that passed my lips and to drink water till I turned into a human aquarium? What choice did I have? I couldn't face the class if I stayed fatter than Andrea. "Fine. The toilet too."

"But about Weight Whippers. I absolutely hate the idea."

"What!" I growled. "I thought the toilet bowl deal included Weight Whippers. Aw gees, Mom, don't you understand? I have to lose weight!"

Patricia looked up from her plate. "No you don't."

"Shut up, Patricia. What do you know!"

She immediately sank into herself, her shoulders slumping. "There's no call for that, Lauren." Mom sat for a while doing mouth exercises. "Since this seems so important to you . . . how's this for a compromise? You're due for a physical. If Dr. Worden thinks Weight Whippers is a good idea for you, I'll let you go. I'll even throw in the money for it."

I hated the idea of seeing the doctor even more than cleaning the toilet bowl. You have to undress for him and then he pokes around your body — a light in your ear, a popsicle stick down your throat, and a stethoscope all over your chest. Maybe he'd even decide it was time to give me a booster shot. "Aw, Dr. Worden!" I groaned.

"There's no discussion. We'll go by his decision and that's that."

After supper I called Stephanie. I didn't mention Weight Whippers. Not yet. I needed to get back on her good side. "So how did the tournament go?"

"What do you care? You hate basketball," she grumbled.

"I do not. I'm just not good at it, that's all. I cut out last night's scores from the newspaper, Steph. Did you know you were third-high scorer?"

"Really?" She was sounding a lot friendlier already.

"Yup. And you know what else?"

"What?"

"I think we should video one of your games."

"Why? You never watch me play."

"True. But haven't you ever wondered what you look like when you do a lay-up . . . backwards?"

"Basketball season is over as of today. If you'd really read the article, you'd know we're bantam champs."

Okay, so I'd only skimmed the piece. She'd caught me. There was a pause, and then I could almost hear her smile.

"Nice try, though, Lauren."

Mom got me an appointment with Dr. Worden after school on Monday. I'd forgotten how short and round and homely he looked. Dr. Worden would never understand wanting to be thin.

He peered into my ear through his little hammer. When he switched to the other one, he noticed my scabs. "Mmm-mmm, I didn't think anybody wore clip-on earrings these days."

"I don't. Those were special ones."

"Well, you know enough to stop wearing them, I hope. Lauren, you have to be good to your body. It's the only one you'll ever have."

"Uh-huh," I answered as I watched him grab a wide popsicle stick from a big glass jar.

"So your mom says you want to join Weight Whippers," he said as he stuck the stick down my throat.

"Uh, wuh wuh ooze eight," I told him.

"Just say 'Aw' please."

"Awwwwww!"

He nodded, removing the stick. "Losing weight is really hard. Deep breaths, please." He placed his stethoscope on my back. "And again." He stuck it between the hospital gown and my chest now. "And again. That's great," he said after a few more breaths.

He looked over my file. "You're not due for a booster till next year." Now he peered at me through his thick swirly glasses, and frowned. For the first time I noticed he had nice, kind of teddy bear eyes. "Let me just show you something."

He took a pink folder from his desk and opened it on my lap. "This is a growth chart for girls." He pointed a stubby finger at a curve. "Between the ages of eleven and thirteen, can you see how steep the weight increase is?"

I nodded.

"That means kids your age gain a lot of weight quickly during this time. Now look over here at the height chart. See, the line's not nearly as steep."

"So what?"

"This means that kids your age often encounter a chubby stage just before they shoot up."

"I'm already taller than my grandmother."

Dr. Worden raised his eyebrows. "You've got a couple of inches on me too." He shook his head. "But that doesn't mean you've stopped growing. And if you diet," he shook a chubby pointer finger at me, "you may actually hinder that growth." He frowned as he stared at me for a moment. "I'd rather see you a little bit heavier at this stage of your life. It's healthier."

"But I don't want to be fat right now!" I told him.

"All right. Get dressed and join your mother and me in the other room."

I watched as he walked into the other office. He didn't understand. How could he? He was old, he had a bald spot. I quickly threw my clothes on and followed him.

There he sat smiling, pictures of his kids propped up all over his desk. Looked like he'd been married forever — why would he care about losing weight? I want to look good! I felt like screaming at him.

"Mrs. Dreyburgh, there is nothing worse for your health than yo-yo dieting . . . "

Here we go, I thought.

" . . . and as I explained to Lauren, she could still shoot up in height so she may slim out naturally . . . but there's nothing wrong with joining a good health club. As far as dieting goes, though . . . "

Oh, right! I folded my arms across my chest and rolled my eyes.

Dr. Worden shook his head and sighed. "Lauren, it's just that at your age you should be too busy having a good time to count calories and fat grams.

You should be climbing every mountain."

"And following every stream," I grumbled.

"Lauren!" Mom snapped.

"That's all right," Dr. Worden told her, and turned to me again, smiling. "So you get the idea, Lauren. I'd rather you didn't diet, period."

"I'm losing weight no matter what you guys say," I snapped.

"We—ll . . ." Hesitating, Dr. Worden turned back to Mom. "If Lauren's really set on losing a little weight, Weight Whippers isn't the worst program she could follow. It incorporates nutrition and behaviour modification therapy . . ."

"You're not suggesting she should sign up, are you?" Mom asked, shocked.

"Yes, I am. I'd rather she joined Weight Whippers than do it on her own."

Hey! Let's hear it for Dr. Teddy Bear! Hip hip hooray!

"I guess it's got to be better than what she's come up with so far. Those earrings were terrible," Mom told him as though I wasn't in the room.

"There's another crazy gimmick every time you open a magazine or turn on the TV," Dr. Worden agreed. He smiled at me. "So you promise now, Lauren? Only a little, and not too quickly?" His teddy-bear eyes stared at me through the thick swirly glass.

I nodded. Just twenty pounds, I thought.

Twenty pounds and I'll be a knockout.

"At least with Weight Whippers, her weight loss will be closely monitored," he continued. "It's when teenagers starve themselves on their own crazy diets, that I really worry."

Chapter 10

"Andrea, do you mind? You're shaking the table!" I looked up from my notebook on day one of my official Weight Whipper diet. It was going on the fifth week of rabbit food for Andrea. She stopped bouncing her leg up and down. Now her fingers drummed instead. "What's your problem anyway? Why don't you eat your lunch?"

"I just feel restless, that's all." She stood up. "I'm going for a walk." She scooped up her backpack and took off.

"But you haven't eaten . . . " Andrea was already gone. "Oh fine, see you later," I said softly to no one. My eyes returned to the page opened in front of me.

Cereal	1 fat	4 fibre	1 bread
Milk	5 fat	0 fibre	1 dairy
Banana	0 fat	4 fibre	1 fruit

My breakfast, I smiled. This was great. I had at least twenty-four more grams of fat to eat the rest of the day. I fingered the fuzzy-people stickers stuck to the cover. Then I wrote down my lunch.

"What are you doing?" Stephanie grumbled as she sat down. It was a standard Stephanie apology.

I smiled, relieved that she would eat with me again. "You don't want to know."

"Aw, something to do with losing weight." Steph shook her head.

"Uh-huh. While you were winning the basketball championship, I went to a Weight Whippers meeting — "

"No, no!" Stephanie made a cross with her fingers as if to ward off vampires.

"Do you want to know or not?"

"Go on."

"I record everything that I eat in my food diary." I held up the little booklet. "Then I look up the fat and fibre content in this guide and mark it down. I also mark down what food group they belong to so I eat a healthy balance." I sipped at my glass of water.

"If I had to do all that, I just wouldn't bother eating," Stephanie said as she watched me.

I studied her for a second and then noticed the food piled in front of her. "Hey, you want me to look up your lunch?"

"No."

"I'll just do the fat. A tuna sandwich is, let's see, bread — two grams. And tuna salad is . . . Do you know if the tuna was packed in water?"

Stephanie sucked in her cheeks. "I should have eaten with the team again."

"Did your mom use real mayonnaise or light?" I flicked through my book now.

"Laurennn."

"It's the mayonnaise that's the killer."

"I don't want to know! I told you already."

"Oh . . . Oh, sorry."

Stephanie didn't answer.

"C'mon, Steph, you like reading the ingredients off the boxes."

She tore into her sandwich. "It's not the same," she mumbled as she chewed. "I happen to like mayonnaise."

"Don't be mad, Steph, because listen, this weekend's Easter, right?"

"Uh-huh."

I grinned. "Well, after we finish our 'Barbie's Adventures in Slime,' we can start work on an eggs-traordinary idea I have for a video."

"Oh yeah? What?" Stephanie leaned forward so I could tell her all about it.

"Hurry up, the blood's rushing to my head," Stephanie said as I drew the second eye at the bottom of her chin. She sat in a chair, leaning way over the back so that her head hung upside down.

"One more second. I just need to fix Eggbert's eyelash. There, that's better." I covered up Stephanie's real eyes and nose with a tea towel, so that only her chin and mouth showed. Great egg-face I'd given her! Cartoon eyes with black irises and exaggerated lashes stared back at me. The pencilled-in two-dot nose twitched as her real mouth pulled down in a smile. Yyess! This should work. "Say something," I told her.

Steph wiggled her mouth up and down. "Easter's here and I'm very egg-cited."

I snorted. It was that big mouth stretching into strange directions that was so hilarious. "That's great." I chuckled, whipping off the tea towel. "Okay, sit up and rest for a minute while I get a big blanket to cover the tops of our faces."

On the way to the linen closet I stopped in the bathroom to check out my own egg-face. It wasn't easy. I needed to cover my eyes and nose and turn my head to the side a bit to try to get the upside-down effect. Then I had to peek through my fingers to actually see. My egg eyes stretched skinny across my chin, almost shifty looking. My egg nose, pencilled-nostrils in an upside-down U, looked piglike. But just like Steph's, my mouth seemed huge in the small egg head, so stretching it produced the funniest face.

As I grabbed a blanket from the shelf I called to Nan. "We're ready. Can you come and film us?"

"All righty." Nan followed me back into the living room. She frowned as she lifted her purple glasses to the top of her head, picked up the camera and peered into the viewfinder. "I just look in this little window and press this button?"

"Uh-huh, just a minute." I lay down upside down

on the couch as close as possible to Steph, draping the blanket around our faces to cover everything but our mouths and chins. "Okay, go."

"Hi, everybody! I'm Eggward." I forced the corners of my mouth down hard to form a smile for my chin-man.

Nan started chuckling.

"And I'm Eggbert," Stephanie continued.

"And we're here to offer you a few suggestions for a safer, happier Easter." I leaned my chin-head toward hers. "One: Absolutely no head banging!" I yelled as we both bounced our chins up and down.

"Two: No sitting on walls," Eggbert added. "Remember what happened to Humpty Dumpty."

"Three: If the chicken decides to cross the road, make sure you look both ways before you follow it."

"And, here's an idea. Why not try dyeing your cereal this year for a change, *not* eggs," Eggbert called.

"Much safer." I nodded Eggward's head to agree.

"And our final message: Get plenty of *egg*cersize!"

It was all really corny, but combined with the strange mouth movements our "Eggs Men" video was a riot.

That Sunday after turkey dinner Stephanie came over and we all sat around watching it. Patricia nearly choked on her chocolate laughing at it. And for once Mom loved Stephanie's slightly ghoulish ending. It was brilliant. We bumped into each other's chins hard, stopped the camera, then filmed two broken eggs on the floor.

"Happy Easter from Eggbert." Extreme closeup of an egg yolk.

"And Eggward." Extreme closeup of another yolk.

THE END, the little white piece of paper on the screen read.

I glanced over at Patricia, who had just polished off the head of her chocolate bunny. Ooooh, chocolate . . .

"Why don't you just have a taste of that special cream egg I bought you?" Nan said. Maybe she'd noticed me drooling. "Easter only comes once a year."

"Does every holiday need to focus on food?" I muttered. It was what Kate Luzinsky had asked yesterday at my second Weight Whippers meeting. Three pounds less, I'd weighed. I didn't dare nibble on chocolate today. "The video was supposed to be my contribution to a non-food celebration."

"Aw, you're just being obnoxious," Stephanie said.

"And you're being unsupportive!" I told her.

That Tuesday the Aerobics Army stood in formation on the exercise floor as Andrea stepped onto the scale. Sergeant Praying Mantis fiddled with the sound system while she waited for us.

Another four pounds for Andrea. One more than I'd lost. She swayed as she stepped down.

"You okay?" I asked as I steadied her. "Maybe you're coming down with something."

"I'm fine." Andrea shut her eyes for a moment. "We'd better join the class. Exercise will clear my head."

Later when we finished our Select Women routine, Mrs. Partington picked us up and I got her to drop me off at Stephanie's.

"I made a salad for supper," Stephanie said as she took me into the kitchen. "There's your water." She pointed to a filter jug in the middle of the table and poured herself a glass of her own.

"You can have Coke," I told her. "You don't have to deprive yourself."

Stephanie raised her eyebrows for a moment. "Oh sure. And I can have french fries and lasagna and pizza with chocolate cake for dessert. But then you'd watch me like a hungry wolf. Or you'd do that thing with your mouth."

I pursed my lips together, chewing at the insides of my mouth.

"That's it, that's the thing!" She pointed at my mouth.

I chewed even harder.

"See what I mean? No thank you. I'll just have

water and salad. Nobody can accuse *me* of being unsupportive. "

The next Monday marked the end of week two of my new lifestyle change. That second week I'd lost two pounds and Andrea had lost three. How could she keep it up? She weighed four pounds less than I did now, and she was at least half an inch taller.

At Weight Whippers Kate Luzinsky had told us to work at eating in a relaxed environment and to try chewing and savouring our food more. Sitting in the cafeteria now with Steph, I closed my eyes and took four deep breaths before even taking my lunch from the bag.

"Now what?" Steph said when she noticed.

"I'm just doing a little relaxation technique. I'm not bothering you, am I?"

"I guess not." She eyed me suspiciously.

I took a bite of my lettuce and tomato in a pita, put the sandwich down and began chewing as I stared at my watch. Five seconds, ten seconds, fifteen, twenty . . . I swallowed and then waited as another ten seconds passed. I drank some water and glanced over at Stephanie.

In just thirty seconds she'd eaten an entire thermos cup of Spaghetti-Os. "Wow!" I commented.

"Whaaaat?"

"Oh, nothing." I knew better than to say anything more.

"C'mon, out with it. How many fats?"

"The Spaghetti-Os? Less than five, don't worry. Really, it doesn't have anything to do with you." I took another bite of my pita, lay it down, and timed my chewing again. Thirty seconds later I took another bite.

"Aw, what are you doing now, Lauren?" Stephanie sputtered.

"I'm timing my eating. Half a minute for each bite, that's my goal this week."

"At that rate I'll be finished my whole lunch by the time you've eaten half your sandwich."

"You're right. Now if your Spaghetti-Os had any kind of fibre in them, you would chew a little longer naturally."

"Lauren!"

"Hey, I wasn't going to bring it up. Only you asked."

The third week of my diet, I lost two pounds. Andrea lost five.

"How many does that make, Andrea? Altogether I mean?" I asked as she stepped off the scale.

"Huh? How many does what make?"

"You know, pounds."

"I lost five."

"I know that! I saw the scale."

Andrea turned to me. Why was she so spaced out? I looked her up and down. She never wore dresses any more. Now her standard was baggy jeans and a man's shirt, and for the gym, a sweat suit. Was it my imagination, or did that sweat suit just hang on her? Her neck looked kind of sinewy. She didn't look solid any more — she looked like something long and breakable, maybe one of those little crystal animal figurines, a giraffe or a deer. When had she changed?

Andrea stared. Her eyes looked like large blue bubbles. Her cheekbones stuck out too, so her eyes seemed sort of hollow. Was she looking at me? I turned to see if there was someone else behind me. No. Maybe she was just looking inside her own head.

"Andrea, how much weight have you lost since you started dieting?" I repeated, saying each word slowly.

Still she stared an extra moment.

"Andrea?"

"I don't know. Forty?"

"Forty! When are you going to stop?" I asked. "Andrea, I'm talking to you."

She looked over at the aerobics floor. "Stop exercising?"

"No, dieting. Aren't you thin enough yet?"

Suddenly Andrea's eyes focussed sharply. "Never. You can never be thin enough."

I thought about that as I followed her baggy sweat suit over to the gym floor.

"Does Andrea eat with you?" Mom asked me that night at supper.

I was spooning salsa on my baked potato. The salsa counted as a vegetable and saved me from using fat. "Huh? Andrea? Sure, she sits at our table every day. Why?"

"Oh, well, Brenda wanted me to check. She caught Andrea scraping her supper into the garbage the other day. Now she's watching to make sure Andrea eats something."

Well, I thought, she sat with us, and she cut and arranged her carrots and celery at our table every day, but did she actually eat? That was a different question. "Maybe she had an upset stomach," I suggested.

"I don't know. Brenda's really worried about her. She wants Andrea to stop dieting. She thinks Andrea's too thin."

"You can never be thin enough." Andrea's words popped out before I even thought about them.

"The expression is 'You can never be too thin or too rich,' if you really want to know," Mom told me, frowning. "But that's all nonsense, Lauren, because the one thing money can't buy is health." She touched my hand. "Now, you pay attention to your friend, and tell me if Andrea really seems healthy."

Chapter 11

That Saturday marked week four of my diet. Down one, the Weight Whippers attendant told me. Only one pound! But Kate said that was normal. "You reach a plateau at some point and you need to be extra careful not to slip into bad habits. For instance, did anyone measure their cereal in the morning?"

I'd never done that but Kate showed us how much bran cereal actually made up a serving. She poured it into a big bowl and swirled it in front of our noses as she walked between the rows of chairs. "If you filled this bowl, you'd actually have three servings."

Who would want to? I thought. The bran cereal's little brown pellets reminded me of rabbit droppings.

Then Kate dumped the droppings in a smaller bowl and the cereal reached right to the brim. "Measure your food the first few times and then if you like, stick to the same plate or bowl so that you can gauge by eye how much food will equal one serving."

I was amazed.

Sunday morning I measured my cereal and discovered I was eating two and a half servings of Oats 'n' Bran. No wonder I had reached a plateau. I searched around in the cupboard and found my old baby bowl. Perfect. One serving.

Presentation week for our May speeches started the next day. After eating a baby bowl full of Oats 'n' Bran, I walked with Stephanie to school. A restless, edgy Stephanie.

"You'll do fine," I told her. "You worked hard. And just think. In another half hour it will all be over."

Stephanie sneered at me.

I smiled back. Asking for the first time slot had been my idea. Steph knew her topic cold. There had been no point in delaying. Even so, as she stepped to the front I felt more nervous for her than I ever felt making my own speeches.

"The actor who played Frankenstein needed to show up four hours earlier on set for make-up call. Every morning at two . . . " Stephanie said without a breath.

Slow down, I thought as she rattled on.

" . . . make-up artists would build up his forehead with special skin putty, letting it set as they oiled his hair . . . "

Look up! Eye contact, eye contact!

" . . . and shaped his other scars. Um . . . um . . . "

Shading next. Talk about the shading, I

mouthed at her, but it was no use. She continued to stare at the floor.

"Then they . . . um, shaded and coloured his skin. Um . . . "

Somehow she muddled through, finishing with vampire make-up. At the end of her presentation she finally looked up and smiled, probably because she was so relieved to have it over. But the effect was perfect. The plastic fangs I'd convinced her to wear showed for the first time, and the class roared. She probably only would have got a B– without that ending. A+ is what I marked on her evaluation. Of course, I'd have given A+ even without the fangs.

That baby bowl of cereal I'd eaten in the morning carried me through Steph's presentation and three more. Then the bowling balls rolled through my stomach. To make matters worse, I hadn't brought a lunch and was planning to grab a salad. Only it was lasagna day at the cafeteria. I sniffed the air. "Tomato sauce, beef, cheese," I mumbled.

"Oh, have some. It won't kill you," Stephanie told me. "I've given my last presentation for the year. Let's celebrate."

"I don't know . . . There's so much fat in the cheese and the meat."

"So have less." She placed a lasagna dish on her own tray.

I stared at it, watching the cheese still bubbling

up from beneath the sauce. I thought of Andrea, who was at least five pounds thinner than I was by now, even though I'd lost weight too. I needed to catch up to her. I chewed my lip and thought about Weight Whippers — a lifetime struggle, one of the members had called the programme. Did I want to say no to my favourite food for the rest of my life? "No!" I finally said out loud, and asked Mrs. Fatawa for a serving of lasagna too.

Back at the table I took out my little book with the fat and fibre measurements. Lasagna wasn't listed. I had to look up noodles and then the minced beef and the mozzarella cheese. The tomato sauce didn't count as anything. I stared at my plate.

"Eat up. It's delicious," Stephanie said through a mouthful.

I picked up my fork and then frowned.

"What's wrong now?"

"I don't know how to measure the serving size."

"Huh?"

"Well four ounces of beef counts as five grams of fat, one ounce of cheese has four. One cup of noodles counts as one carbohydrate."

Stephanie made a face. "Why don't you just weigh everything?"

I lifted the plate with one hand, raised and lowered it, eyeing it sideways.

"I was kidding!" she shrieked. "Sheesh, you're getting as bad as Andrea."

I put down the plate. "The size of my fist is the right size for a meat serving." I made a fist over my square of lasagna and then carefully trimmed a little off two sides. And then I dug my fork into my first mouthful of lasagna in over a month. The cheese hung down in soft strings, just the way I liked it. Mmmm. I closed my eyes and tasted. It was warm and saucy with just the right touch of spice.

Andrea sat down then. I opened my eyes again. Andrea barely perched on the edge of her chair. She seemed to be staring at my lasagna.

"Are you staying, or what?" Stephanie demanded. "Where's your lunch?"

Andrea stood up like a bird frightened from a wire. Then she perched again. "I didn't bring any."

Eyes closed, I savoured my third bite. I opened my eyes and glanced at her. *She never eats with us any more* . . . The truthful answer to my mother's question finally hit me. *Did* Andrea look healthy? Hmm.

"Andrea, why don't you have some of Lauren's lasagna? She can't possibly eat it all," Steph suggested, gesturing to the L-shape I had cut from my piece.

"No!" She flew up again as though afraid of it.

"She hasn't touched it," Steph continued.

"Here, sit down. I'll even get you a plate."

"I can't," she said flatly. Then took off.

"You did that on purpose," I growled at Stephanie as I watched Andrea hurry out of the cafeteria.

"Whaaat? I was just offering her some lunch. You said you didn't want it, right?" Stephanie forked some lasagna into her mouth, annihilating it in seconds. "Whatever happened to the sweet polite Andrea we used to know, anyway?"

"Don't be like that, Steph," I said. "Andrea's working so hard to lose weight. You have no idea what a pain it is to exercise and diet all the time. It takes up your whole life."

Stephanie stopped shovelling food into herself for a moment and looked me square in the eyes. "Oh, I think I have a pretty good idea."

I knew that tone in her voice. I knew that look. Before we got into an argument I decided it was time to change the subject. "So, Steph, Mother's Day is this Sunday. Did you buy anything yet?"

"No, you?" Stephanie started into her lasagna again.

"I don't have a cent. But you know what?"

"What?" she mumbled through a mouthful.

"After the rave success of our 'Easter Eggs' video, I think it might be time for a return of the Eggs Men."

"Yeah! That's a great idea." Steph put her fork down. "And you know, I have the perfect prop."

After school, back at my house, we set up the tripod for Nan, and Stephanie explained how we were going to use the prop.

"Uh-huh." Nan's sides shook. "That's good, that's really good," she said, wiping her eyes beneath her purple frames. "You kids sure have a warped imagination."

We got into position on the couches and wrapped the blanket around the tops of our heads.

"Hi, I'm Eggbert," Steph said, frowning hard so that Eggbert appeared to be smiling.

"And I'm Eggward." I wiggled my chin.

"Remember Humpty Dumpty sat on a wall and had a great fall?" Eggbert asked.

"And remember when Eggbert and I head-banged together?" Eggward interrupted.

"Well, all the king's horses and all the king's men put us together again — "

"So that we could wish you a Happy Mother's Day," Eggward finished.

"Happy Mother's Day," we both hollered together.

"M is for the money that you give me," I sang.

"O is for the omelettes that you made me," Eggbert continued.

"Your mom made you omelettes?" I cried. "My mother never whipped or beat us."

146

"Sure."

Now Eggbert recited: *"Eggs in the carton, eggs in the nest, eggs in the frying pan z'what I like best."*

"Oh really, Eggbert, I eggs-pected more from you."

Nan groaned as I continued the song: *"M is that I really could use more!"*

"More money?" Eggbert asked.

"Much more money. Then I could have bought Mom a real present," Eggward answered.

"Put 'em all together, they spell Mo-o-om," Eggbert and Eggward sang together, *"the word that means the world to me!"*

Nan stopped the camera at this point and lowered the special prop which was tied by its neck to a ribbon. She held it as she re-started the camera.

"Mo-o-om!" Eggbert kissed the prop.

"You sure she's not the chicken that crossed the road?" Eggward said. "Hey, it's my mom." He kissed it. "Mo-o-om!"

"Mo-o-om!" Both of us I kissed it now. Extreme close up of "Mom," a classic yellow rubber chicken, with skinny legs ending in long orange claws. Mom's eyes were tight black slits and her mouth opened as though in a final last gasp.

We threw off the blanket and sat right-side-up on the couch. In seconds we had the video rewound, and popped it into the VCR. Our performance, I had to admit, was amazing. "Gotta hand it to you," I told Steph. "The rubber chicken makes the video."

"Oh, I don't know. I like all the jokes you made up."
Steph wiped at Eggbert's face with a washcloth.

"What a team, eh?" I dipped my washcloth into
some cold cream and destroyed Eggward.

That was the best we got along all week. Tuesday
was exercise day as usual, and Steph headed home
in disgust with Emily Urbaniak while I power
walked to the gym with Andrea. I had to. I'd even
booked my presentation for the very last day to give
myself the most time. But still, this week was my
last chance to lose weight.

I bicycled twenty minutes on the exercycle after
Tuesday and Thursday's aerobics classes. When
Sergeant Praying Mantis asked if we'd had
enough, I shouted "No!"

At home I vacuumed the family room to rock
music and scrubbed the toilet extra hard. All to
burn more calories and get down from that plateau.

"Nothing tastes as good as slim feels," Kate Luzinsky told us on Saturday at Weight Whippers.
It was the end of week four for me. "Remember
that when you reach for a bag of chips. Better yet,
tape that motto to your fridge and read it before
you eat!"

"Amen," Charlene the cheesecake lady said.

"Mmm hmm," Her friend Doris agreed.

"Now I have a happy-face bookmark to award," Kate announced. "One of our members has lost ten pounds. Would you put your hands together for Lauren Dreyburgh!"

Chapter 12

Finally it was Monday — my speech day. I slipped into exercise leggings. No pulling, stretching or yanking and no lying on the bed. They just slipped on. I threw on my Select Women T-shirt and stood on my bed to see the effect in the mirror over my dresser. Were my thighs still a touch heavy? I had to crouch to see my whole body in the mirror so it was hard to say. The bed bounced slightly. The flab on my thigh jiggled. I sighed.

"Never mind. Ten pounds, right on target," I told my mirror image. Nothing could feel this good.

I pulled on one of Dad's sweat suits. Should I stuff it? Nah, the stuffing might be awkward to take out in front of the class.

"I made some oatmeal," Nan announced when I walked into the kitchen.

She was making me breakfast again. Uh-oh.

"Did you put cream in?" I asked sharply.

"No. I made it with water, and no brown sugar. You can add it yourself."

"Good." I tasted some. Ugh! "Do we have any apples?"

"In the fridge."

I took one and slivered it up onto the oatmeal. Then I sprinkled on some cinnamon. It still needed brown sugar, but I didn't add any. Not today. I wanted to feel especially good about myself today, and so far things were definitely going my way. Ten pounds! I'd set out to lose them and I did!

There was nothing I couldn't achieve once I put my mind to it. I marched out to school after breakfast singing the Weight Whippers jingle under my breath. "Life is great when you lose that weight!" Stephanie met me near the school. "So don't wait, to make that date!" I sang louder. Then I flung my arms out in the air and finished with a flourish: "To join Weight Whippers!"

"Only you could be in this good a mood before a class speech," Stephanie commented. "Nervous, Lauren?"

"No, no, no, no, no, no," I continued to sing to the obnoxious tune of the jingle. When Kim strolled by, she made her usual arrow eyebrows. I gave her a big smile. Jay was trailing behind her. I gave him a big wink.

I didn't need any cards or notes for this speech. I skipped up to the front of the class, made eye contact with Steph, Jay, Carlos and Ms Smyrnios, and grinned.

"Weighing in at one thousand four hundred pounds, Jon Brower Minnoch was the world's heaviest person. When he sat around the house, he *really* sat around the house." I paused for the snickers and giggles. "It was rumoured that he was baptised at Marineland." I looked toward Andrea, thinking she would enjoy these jokes now that she was thin, but she shifted around in her chair without looking at me. I cleared my throat. "When he died he was placed in a piano case and hoisted by crane into his grave." More giggles.

I actually didn't think that was so funny. I took a few deep breaths while the snickers died. "I used to worry that I would become a piano-case person. I know I wasn't that fat, but a lot of older heavy people I know say they were thin when they were my age. And well, I wasn't. I'd try to diet on my own, but I couldn't stick with it. I felt out of control. It was a scary feeling. Till I went on a program, a lifelong program."

I sounded like Kate now as I told them about fat and fibre counting, food diaries, power walking, weight plateaus and measuring food. As I spoke about it, I became amazed all over again that I could have done all that. When I got to the end, I stripped off the sweats to my exercise tights and T-shirt. "Nobody needs to stay fat. I took control of my life, and anyone else can too. All it takes is a little willpower. Thank you very much."

"Whoo hoo!" Stephanie cheered. There were wolf

whistles from the back. I smiled as I headed to my seat. The applause continued.

Andrea didn't clap and didn't look my way. I couldn't understand her. I was really telling our story. Why wasn't she clapping?

"Well," Ms Smyrnios said, "That sounds as if it took more than just a little willpower. Good speech, Lauren."

I shrugged my shoulders. "Thanks."

"Andrea? You're up next."

No wonder Andrea wouldn't look at me. Why hadn't she asked me for help with her presentation? Well, now that she was thin she probably didn't need it. No one would laugh at her figure, that was for sure.

As Andrea drifted to the front, Jay and Matt jostled each other, talking and laughing about something. Andrea stood at the front now, swaying back and forth on her heels. She was wearing a pair of droopy jeans and a large striped shirt. Was it Roy's? Her face had lost its soft puffy pinkness. Tendons showed through the skin of her neck. She looked thin, really thin. . . . Again my mother's question came back to me: Did she seem healthy?

"Did you forget your cue cards?" Ms Smyrnios asked when Andrea didn't start right away.

"Mmm, no, I didn't make any. I want to talk about the proper care of a horse." Andrea's large eyes looked ready to pop, but they never held anyone else's gaze, not even for a moment. Instead they floated, never stopping to look at any one thing. It was as though she had written notes on things in the classroom, on the floor, the desks, over the blackboards and she needed to glance at each note before continuing.

The class became quiet, waiting. Jay put his baseball cap on his head, pulling the brim over his eyes. Then he stretched back with his hands behind his head and pretended to snore. Ms Smyrnios walked to the back of the room and snatched off his hat.

"Some kids only want a horse so they can ride it." Andrea looked at the wall for a moment and stopped talking. She curled and uncurled each one of her fingers against her thumb. I could hear Matt humming the theme tune from "The Twilight Zone."

"Shhh!" I hissed at him.

Andrea didn't seem to notice, and finally started again. "But there's a lot more to owning your own horse than . . . " Suddenly, bizarrely, Andrea dropped — like a sandbag someone had poked a hole in and all the insides had spilled out.

Ms Smyrnios gasped and rushed to the front. She knelt down and as Andrea's eyes flicked open, gently pushed her shoulders to keep her lying down. "Don't get up, you've fainted," Ms Smyrnios said. She motioned to Carlos. "Run and get a glass of water from the staff room!"

"I'm okay, I'm fine," Andrea said, lifting her head again.

"I'm sure you are. But it's almost lunch time. Perhaps your blood sugar's a little low. Did you eat breakfast this morning?"

Andrea's eyes narrowed as she sat up. "Yes."

"I have an arrowroot biscuit in my desk. Maybe you can just nibble it for some strength."

"No!" Andrea snapped.

Ms Smyrnios stared at her for a moment.

"I — I mean — I think I'd be sick." Andrea tried a small smile and shrugged her shoulders.

Ms Smyrnios nodded. Carlos returned with the water then and Andrea drank it all down.

"Lauren, would you take Andrea to the office?" Ms Smyrnios asked.

"Why?" Again Andrea spoke too sharply, but she quickly covered up with a smile. "Really, Ms Smyrnios, I'm fine."

"I would like the office to get in touch with one of your parents."

"But . . . " Andrea was ready to argue.

I tried warning her with my eyes. Couldn't she see? Everything she said was calling more attention to herself.

"Come on," I told her, grabbing her elbow to help her up. It was like holding onto a broomstick. We walked out the door.

Andrea clicked her tongue. "I want to give my

speech." She stopped and I had to keep her from going back. "Oh, why can't she let me get it over with?" Her voice sounded desperate now.

"If you'd eaten the stupid cookie, she might have," I snapped.

"You're right."

I pulled her along again.

"You know what they're all like." She marched as she spoke. "They want me to eat and eat and eat. Have breakfast, have lunch, here's a cookie." Her footsteps hammered the rhythm of her words. "They like me as Andrea the good little butterball. Then they have somebody to make fun of."

Like Jon Brower Minnoch, I thought. *When he sat around the house, he really sat around the house . . . baptised at Marineland . . .* It seemed so easy to make fun of fat people. I guess I was just as bad as everyone else, telling those jokes.

We passed the cafeteria now. I could smell frying onions and hamburgers.

"Isn't that disgusting?" Andrea asked, wrinkling her nose.

It was a heavy greasy smell. I nodded, agreeing with her. "They always make such fattening foods."

"Yeah. And then they tell you to eat fruits and vegetables." Andrea shook her head. "You have to be so strong to resist food. It's all around you. It's all anybody thinks about."

"But you've done great on your diet," I said.

Maybe now you should stop, I wanted to add, but Andrea interrupted me.

"You think so?" Her lips lifted slightly with just a hint of a smile. "It's so hard to have control over your weight. Especially when everyone's always trying to get you to eat."

Now we were at the office. Andrea grabbed me suddenly and stopped us from moving. "I can't call my mother. You understand, don't you? She wants me fat again." She looked straight into my eyes. "You're my best friend, Lauren. Don't tell, okay?"

"But Andr— "

She let go of me and headed for the front door. I watched her walk away. Should I stop her? Should I tell? She'd fainted, after all. Didn't that mean that she was sick?

This was so hard. The real reason Andrea thought I was her best friend was because I was her *only* friend. And that was so sad, because I didn't really think of her as a friend at all.

But I did understand her, and I knew I could never snitch. "Andrea! Wait!" I called to her, hoping to convince her to talk to her mother herself.

No answer. The door swung closed.

Chapter 13

I didn't go back to the classroom. Ms Smyrnios would ask about Andrea, and I knew I couldn't lie. Since it was so close to lunch, I headed for the cafeteria and sat down at our regular table.

"That was a great speech," Kim told me when she passed. "Imagine, fourteen hundred pounds. What a pig that guy must have been!" She tossed her hair back and then sauntered over to the guys' table.

A pig . . . That sounded so mean, but I guess I'd called him a whale . . . Pretty scary to think that people made fun of a person because he was fat even after he was dead. When Steph sat down I asked her, "Did you know Jon Brower Minnoch was married?"

"Nope. I don't remember you saying that in your speech."

"Well, I didn't. It — it didn't really fit. Do you suppose they had kids?"

"How would I know?" Steph dumped her lunch bag on the table, and her apple rolled away. She caught it before it went off the edge. "What do you care anyway?"

"Because. Just imagine your father dying and being buried in a piano case and everyone laughing when the crane hoisted him into his grave."

"Well, no one would be mean enough to laugh out loud at the cemetery. They'd probably save their yuks for later." Stephanie crunched into her apple. "Anyway, I bet the kids would be used to it. People must have laughed at their father his whole life."

"But that's awful, don't you think?" I took out my container of pumpkin and Synthisweet.

"Uh-huh. Awful." Steph finished the apple and then pitched her core into the garbage. "Hey, did Andrea's mom come and get her?"

I spooned some pumpkin into my mouth. For a moment it tasted sweet, and then a sharp bitterness pinched at my tongue. "Andrea never called her."

Stephanie rolled her eyes.

"She made me promise not to tell, Steph, she said I was her best friend and she begged me and everything."

"Well, isn't that just like Andrea? She needed you again so she said you were her best friend."

"That's just not fair and you know it. Everyone always hates Andrea just because she's fat."

"Oh yeah? If that's true, how come I don't like her any better now that she's skinny?"

"But she's not always so hard to take. You should see her with her brothers. She — "

"C'mon, Lauren, admit it. You wouldn't be friends with her if it weren't for your mother."

"Oh no? At least she understands how hard it is to diet. Not like some people I know who are constantly pigging out in front of me."

"Me? I'm just eating my normal way." Stephanie unwrapped a sandwich and ripped into it. "It's you two who've gone ballistic over this dieting stuff." She sipped from her milk now. "Especially Andrea."

"What do you know?" I snapped, crossing my arms across my chest.

"Maybe nothing. But I think you should at least tell your mother about Andrea fainting. She really looks out of it. What if she *is* sick or something?"

I didn't answer her even though what she said prickled under my skin.

"Okay, okay, Lauren, don't be mad. Let's change the subject." Steph's eyebrows gave me an up and down signal. "Look who's coming through the door."

I turned around in my seat as Jay strode by.

"Notice anything different about him?" Stephanie asked.

He stood in the cafeteria line now and I looked him over from his hair to his hightops. "No," I sighed. "He's still the same old stud muffin."

"Let's try again. Notice anything missing from him?"

"His cap?" I answered. Maybe Ms Smyrnios hadn't given it back yet.

"No — check it out. He's not hanging around with Kim any more." Stephanie poked me in the back. "Lauren, Lauren, this is your big moment in life. You should go up to him, ask him to the mall."

Hmm, I thought, the new slim me . . . What would Jay say? It was too scary. "Nah, I need to lose a little more weight. I want him to see me as a knockout first."

"You look great right now," Stephanie said. "If you ask me, you're just chicken."

Stephanie could be such a pain.

It surprised me that Andrea still showed up for aerobics that day. Maybe she was okay after all. What a relief. After class I decided to try and spend some time with her, seeing as I was her only best friend. And it's not just because of my mother either, I told myself. I really wanted to be a friend to her. I was going to convince her she didn't need to diet any more, and that she should tell her mother she'd fainted at school.

"Hey Andrea, why don't we grab a Coke before we head home."

"A Coke?" she snapped.

"Well, the diet kind, you know. The little coffee shop at the end of the hall must have some."

"Do they have it in cans?" Andrea studied me almost suspiciously.

"How do I know? Why don't we check?"

She followed along, so I took that as a yes. But she just kept staring at the guy behind the counter.

"Psst, look. He's pouring the soft drinks from that nozzle. That means they don't have it in cans."

"So what's the big deal? You like the tinny after-taste of canned pop or something?" I was trying hard to be pals with her, only I was losing it. *You missed a macaroni over there*, I remembered her telling me. Why couldn't she ever let up?

"Sometimes . . . " Andrea lowered her voice now, still watching the guy, "when they run out of diet pop, they switch to regular!"

"No kidding." If Stephanie were here, she'd give me her zombie stare and I could make a face back. "You know, a regular Coke might not be such a bad idea, Andrea. You fainted today, remember. Maybe it's because — "

"Why don't we go to the mall across the street. There's a machine there." The way she snapped out the words, I knew she'd heard me. She just wasn't going to discuss it.

Sure enough, she marched out the door of the fitness building, across the street and into the new Economart Mall. I followed quickly behind her.

I checked around for my sister but didn't see her.

I thought I spotted Jay for a moment, but then realized it was just another tall guy in baggy jeans and a baseball cap. "Hey, slow down, Andrea, where's the machine, anyway?"

"Up the escalator, over there." She pointed.

As we started up I watched the people ahead of us in the mirrored wall. A slim brunette with a pretty face and nice hair. Then a blonde with purple hollows under her cheekbones, and huge blue eyes. Hey, that was Andrea!

I reached up to rake my fingers through my own hair and then it hit me — that brunette was me. The split second in which I saw myself as thin flashed by. I checked out my body again. "Andrea, Andrea, do you think my thighs are heavy?" With my jacket on and my baggy jeans it was hard for me to tell.

Andrea looked up where I was pointing. "No, they're perfect. Mine are like lumps of dough."

I studied her body in that mirror for another quick second, then we were at the next floor and needed to get off. I couldn't tell about her thighs either, but her neck looked like a bird's. We deposited our coins in the soft-drink machine and the Diet Coke lit up to say they were all out. I pressed the button for diet gingerale and clunk, clunk, the can rolled down the chute. I reached out for it. "You're not having any, Andrea?"

"I guess not. I don't like gingerale."

I sipped at my drink. "Well, fine then. Let's go home." We started walking toward the escalator again.

"Hey, I have a better idea. Why don't you come to my house?"

Andrea stepped onto one of the stairs.

"The twins are there, aren't they?" I stepped one level above her and we started moving down.

"Yeah, but Mom and Roy will be out. I promised to make supper so the baby-sitter could go home at the regular time. And you know what?

"What?"

"I can make you the perfect supper. The same one I made on Mother's Day. No fat, very few calories." We both got off the escalator now.

"Well, it *is* really hard always watching Patricia eat. She puts a ton of butter on everything and she never trims the fat off her meat."

"Yuck. And you can help me!"

"Oh? How?" Please, no more sweeping up or working on her speech.

"You can be a witness to my mother that I did eat. She's really ragging at me about that lately."

"Okay. Only I better call Nan from your house."

Mrs. Jansen, the baby-sitter, looked pretty happy to see us when we got to Andrea's. She gathered up her things as Andrea hung up our coats and lined our boots against the wall of the hall closet.

"I'm to tell you there's that special double-fudge ice cream you like so much in the freezer. Be a good girl and have some. You're nothing but a bag of bones, child."

"I will, don't worry!" Smiling, Andrea waved to Mrs. Jansen from the front door. When the baby-sitter reached the end of the block, Andrea's smile dropped and she slammed the door shut. "Another spy," she hissed.

Huh? What did Andrea mean by —

"Andy, Andy! You're home."

We could hear Neil and Noah shrieking as they tumbled from the family room. "Make us flower salad for supper. Please, please, please."

Andrea brightened as she bent down and caught them each in one arm. "You're in luck. That's just what I planned." She kissed Noah and brushed Neil's hair back. "But you have to go play quietly in the basement till I'm ready or I won't be able to make it."

"Sure, Andy, we'll be quiet." They giggled and ran after each other. As they stomped down the stairs the whole house seemed to shake.

Andrea paid no attention. "Brrr, it's cold in here," she said as she closed the door behind them. "Wait till I turn down the air conditioning. Do you want to borrow a sweater?"

"No. I'm fine." I watched as she adjusted the thermostat from twenty-four to twenty-six.

"I'm just going to grab one of Roy's." She came back after a moment wearing a huge cable-knit sweater. Then she rummaged through the fridge for some vegetables.

"Flower salad?" I asked as I watched her run the tines of a fork hard over a carrot.

"I just make the veggies look pretty for everyone." Now she sliced the carrots thin. Each piece turned out to be a little orange daisy.

"Oh, I see. Can I do something?"

"Sure. Get the radishes from the fridge. You can make the roses. And hand me the tomatoes, please."

Supper at Andrea's turned out to be even more fiddly than before. She made rice in chicken bouillon. No butter or fat needed at all, she explained. She grilled a couple of chicken breasts with honey and mustard, then she arranged the carrot daisies, radish roses and tomato tulips over some lettuce leaves. She placed small bunches of parsley in the middle of the rice on each plate. Even her own.

It looked like plenty of vegetables, carbohydrates and protein to me. If she eats like this, she's got to be healthy, I thought. Her mother has nothing to worry about.

Andrea smiled at the twins and me, leaning her head against her hand as we ate. "Oh — I forgot the milk." She jumped up. But the moment she'd poured everyone a glass she asked, "Do you want ketchup on your rice, Neil?" And when he nodded yes she rushed off to get it.

"Is it good?" she asked me when she finally perched back on the edge of her chair.

"Have some yourself, and see," I suggested.

"I am, I am," she answered. She lifted a lettuce leaf with her fingers and nibbled, still watching everyone else.

Noah made a grab for the ketchup and elbowed over his glass of milk. "Sorry," he said as the milk ran down the table onto my leg.

"Don't worry, I've got it," Andrea said as she flew up. She was like Mom after a dozen cups of coffee. Bright, brittle, glassy-eyed. She mopped and wiped and when she finally finished she began scraping plates into the garbage, starting with her own. When had she eaten the rest of her supper?

"Everybody stay sitting. I made dessert this morning. Weight Whippers pudding," she declared as she set parfait glasses in front of us. Then she sat back, smiling, eyes twitching.

"Oh, but there's only four," I said. "You didn't know I was coming. C'mon, have your pudding."

"No!" Andrea snapped.

Neil and Noah looked at her, startled.

"I . . . I mean, no thank you," she said when she noticed their faces. "Sorry, Lauren. It's just that you sounded exactly like my mother."

"She's bugging you that much?"

"Like you wouldn't believe. But you saw me, I ate."

After supper the twins made us watch a Nickelodeon show where these kids had to compete against each other to climb this huge rock. Neil and Noah yelled and cheered, which was normal, but what was worse was Andrea bouncing and fidgeting. She seemed full of some kind of electrical charge and I felt exhausted from dodging the sparks. At the earliest polite moment, I said it was time to go home.

Peace and quiet, I sighed as I walked. What a relief. From a freshly mown lawn, the smell of cut grass drifted up to me. And for some reason it hit me then. *I never did see Andrea eat. Not the chicken. Not the rice. Not the double-fudge ice cream.* She didn't really eat any dinner at all.

That fifth week I lost another pound. Kate Luzinsky asked me how I was doing and suggested that maybe it was time to go on maintenance.

"What do you mean?" I asked.

"Well, for your height, you're thin enough. And you lost that ten pounds a little quickly. Now it's time to start stabilizing."

"But I can't stop losing weight yet! Look at my hips and my thighs. I'm a hippo!"

Kate took a deep breath and shook her head. "Be realistic, Lauren. We all have different shapes."

"But I worked so hard. I can't stop while I still have rhinoceros rump."

Kate chuckled now. "You don't have any such thing. Keep exercising. And while you're stabilizing you may lose another pound or two."

"But I have to lose nine more pounds." Twenty pounds altogether, then I would be a knockout for Jay.

"Nine more pounds for your height? No. You see, you're going by a number instead of what's right for you, what feels best. How do your clothes fit?"

"Good."

"So then let's add another couple of floaters per day and see how you do this week." Kate smiled. "Congratulations, Lauren."

I didn't feel pleased or excited. I felt lost, and definitely not thin enough. I wanted to look in the mirror and see Kim's long legs and slim hips attached to me. Only now I could see that would never happen.

"You're in luck!" Stephanie said on Monday when I explained to her what Kate had told me. "Mom packed your favourite cupcakes today." She passed over a package, taking a banana muffin from her bag for herself.

I took off the cellophane wrapper and breathed in the sweet cake smell. *Nothing tastes as good as slim feels.* Was that really true? I pulled out one of Steph's cupcakes and studied it.

"Here's to no more dieting!" Stephanie touched her muffin to my cupcake in a toast. "Come on, Lauren. Bottoms up."

The rest of my life without cupcakes, and yet with saddlebag hips — it was too much to ask of a person. I closed my eyes and sank my teeth into the cupcake.

Mmm. Smooth chocolatey icing first, then spongy cake. Even my teeth sounded happy as they ground down on the sugar. One, two, three bites and then finally the slippery white centre. I groaned.

Two more bites and the first cupcake was gone. I fingered off the frosting from the side of the cardboard.

"Go on, have the second one," Stephanie offered. She had already finished her muffin. "Just for today. To celebrate."

The second cupcake went down much quicker. I couldn't say how my teeth felt or whether the cream centre felt slippery beneath my tongue. My whole mouth tasted like chocolate after. I licked the crumbs from the package.

"Good, eh?" Stephanie asked.

"The first one was fantastic."

"And the second?"

"I should have left it alone." Now I knew how the cheesecake lady felt on the night of her birthday.

I wrote down the cupcakes in my food diary. Why

had I even touched the wrapper? Why couldn't I have been satisfied with just the first one? I ticked off my floaters for the week. One . . . two . . . three . . . Why, why, why? I carved the checkmarks into the paper with my ballpoint pen. I flipped the page and ticked three more from next week's list. Now I'd done it! Not even a hint of salad dressing for two weeks. And butter on potatoes, forget it! I pushed away my lunch, wishing it was my day to go to the gym, but no, I couldn't even work those cupcakes off.

That night I played with my potato at the dinner table. First I flattened it, then I scraped it into a pile, then I spread it out again. The potato looked colourless except for the peel, which pretty much reminded me of dirt. If I snacked on dirt, would that have a lot of fibre in it? I wondered.

Patricia buttered her potato till a pool of yellow floated over it.

I pushed away my plate. I'd rather have no potato at all than this white smush.

"Eat up, Lauren," Mom told me.

"Maybe you could roll your potato bits up into a snowman," Nan suggested, looking at my plate. "They did that with mashed potatoes on 'Cook with Mike' yesterday."

I frowned at Nan, pulled back my plate and fiddled some more with my potato. Nan and Patricia excused themselves but Mom continued to watch me.

"I want it to stop, Lauren." She leaned forward on her hands.

"What?" I gave up on the potato.

"The dieting."

"Why?"

"You're slim enough, and you're getting obsessed about it, that's why. And — there's something wrong with Andrea."

"There's nothing wrong with Andrea," I said quickly, as though I believed it. But Mom's words prickled under my skin just like Stephanie's had.

"You haven't noticed her behaving strangely?"

"She always acts strange. You know how intense she can get sometimes." That wasn't exactly lying, at least.

"Ms Smyrnios called to make sure Brenda knew Andrea had fainted at school."

Now I felt hot and guilty.

"So Brenda took Andrea to the doctor," Mom went on. "He told her she needed to gain at least two pounds by her next visit."

"Aw, Mom, Andrea doesn't want to gain weight! All her life she's been trying to lose it."

"If Andrea doesn't pick up those two pounds, they will admit her to the hospital."

"The hospital!" I couldn't believe Andrea was *that* sick. "I know she's pretty thin, but Mom, she just wants . . . " What was it Andrea wanted from all this dieting? I had to stop and think. "To be perfect." The words came out in clumsy blocks.

"I know, Lauren. And look what she's done to herself. That's why I want you to stop this .— "

I screeched back my chair. Mom wasn't the one everybody thought was fat. She didn't have to live with thunder thighs or rhinoceros rump.

I started to feel angry with everybody and everything. Especially Andrea. I'd trusted her. I thought she knew what she was doing. As I stomped away from the table Mom's words floated through my mind. *You're slim enough . . .* "I'm slim enough, am I? Well, we'll see about that!"

I grabbed the cordless phone from Patricia's room and keyed in the numbers I'd memorized from the phone book. "Hello, may I speak to Jay?"

Chapter 14

Why is it that everything good happens on one day and everything bad happens on another? Friday, after school, Stephanie helped me pick out a new long-sleeve T-shirt in royal blue, and then we found a pair of the latest Ts scrubbed jeans in a paler blue — and for half price. When I tried the two on together in front of the full-length mirror at the store, I stared at my hips. How bad were they?

"Pretty cool, Lauren," Steph told me. "Jay's going to think you're hot stuff."

At that moment another girl, squeezed into the same kind of jeans, stepped out of the fitting room beside me. She was no rhinoceros rump, but still we looked like Before and After bodies for an EZ-Slim ad.

With round dark eyes she stared at herself, her red lips pursed, her long black hair dangling over her shoulder.

"They're really nice, don't you think?" I told her with a smile. Even stretched tightly over her round bottom, I liked the jeans.

"Yeah. But I wish they fit me as well as they do you."

"Me? Thanks." I wanted to tell her that really I was her size, but that through the magic of a weight-loss program and a gym, I had temporarily slimmed down. Then I realized that, for now, somebody believed in the illusion. I might as well enjoy it.

I am a knockout right now, I told myself in my smaller dresser mirror the next day. Not a Kim exactly, but a knockout nonetheless. *And when I meet Jay at the mall after my Weight Whippers meeting, he's going to realize it all at once in a rush, forget Kim, and beg me to go out with him forever.*

"You're up a pound," Kate told me on Saturday when I got weighed before the meeting.

"What? That can't be right! Are the scales working?" I hated the way my voice sounded, peevish and suspicious like Andrea when she quizzed me about whether the diet soft drinks were really from cans.

"It could be just water gain. Don't worry, Lauren. It's just a number, right?"

The fact that the two piano-case ladies had taken off three pounds each made me feel even worse. If I didn't watch out, they'd end up slimmer than me.

From Weight Whippers I hopped the bus over to the mall. I was to meet Jay by the artificial palm tree near the waterfall. The lights beneath the water turned the falls red, then blue, then green, then purple, and in a cheesy kind of way it could have been a romantic setting.

Except I stood there waiting alone. The small backpack I used as a purse became heavy, so I slipped it to the ground in front of me. The colours of the falls changed at least thirty times, making me feel a little heavier and uglier with each minute that passed.

Finally, forty minutes late, Jay shuffled up to me, hands in his pockets, a big grin on his face. "Hi, Lauren. Nice shirt," he said.

He smelled like bubble gum and he looked so good I didn't even ask why he was late. "Wanna grab some fries?" he asked. "I missed breakfast."

"No . . . That is, I'll just have a drink. I'm full. I mean, I ate breakfast . . . Um, you know what I mean." I slipped on my backpack again.

He nodded, still grinning, and we started walking to the Big Potato. I bought a glass of water for ten cents and Jay got the large cheese curds and gravy special. We sat together, me sipping, Jay wolfing and talking, his mouth slightly open.

"Mom was supposed to wake me at ten only, you know, she went for groceries and totally forgot." He stabbed more fries. "So I slept till noon and the bus came late. I can't wait to turn sixteen so I can drive and not have to wait around for a stupid bus."

At that point a little white bubble of cheese stuck

to his chin. It looked like the inside of a zit. Yuck.

But I love him, I told myself. Love can overlook these things, right? Then he wiped it off with his sleeve and he was back to his good-looking self.

"Wanna check out the CDs?" Jay asked as he dumped his plate in the garbage. "Dozers has a new one out."

"Sure." I smiled warmly at him.

He touched my back, guiding me through the entrance poles. I felt a thrill sizzle through me from my backpack straight through to my heart. Lauren Friessen . . . I tried it out in my mind. Mrs. Jay Friessen . . .

I saw my sister over at the last cash register, chatting with the checkout woman. *Look at me, Look at me, Patricia,* I silently willed. But she was too busy. Besides, could she possibly appreciate the accomplishment of having Jay Friessen stroll alongside me, sometimes even touching me, even if it was only through my backpack?

We headed straight to the CD department and browsed a long time, flipping the hard plastic boxes back. Just the two of us. Kind of romantic, shopping for music together.

"It's in! Look, Lauren." Jay lifted up the plastic box to show me.

"All right!" I said. The price sticker read $21.95 — a month of allowance plus change. I could never understand how any of the kids could afford to collect CDs. Jay looked pretty excited though. "You buying it?" I asked.

Jay's grin stretched broader and he shook his head. He put his arm around me. "I need some batteries for my player though."

The clerk watched us as Jay took a package from the display rack. He laid it on the counter and pulled some bills from his pocket. "Will that be all, sir?"

Jay nodded. I put my hand on his arm, enjoying the feeling of owning that small area of his body. We walked out of the department together.

"My pockets aren't big enough. Mind if I stick the batteries in your backpack, Lauren?"

"Go ahead." I turned slightly and again felt something almost like small electrical shocks coming through my bag.

He took my hand then and I felt warm and light, bubbly and sizzly. Sort of like cotton candy, and yet like lasagna.

I spotted Patricia coming toward us at the front exit. Good, now she'd see us together.

"Hi, Patricia," I called, swinging my held hand forward so she could see.

Patricia's face stayed hard and square. "Excuse me, sir, would you please empty your pockets on the counter for me."

Chapter 15

When Patricia's jaw squares and her eyes take on a certain look, there's no arguing with her. Still, I did. "Patricia. This is Jay. He's my friend. He didn't take anything!"

Patricia wouldn't even answer me. Instead she stared at Jay as he took things from his pockets: a key on one of those little plastic million-dollar-bill chains, some change, a roll of breath mints three-quarters empty, and then nothing. Jay pulled the lining from his pocket to prove it to Patricia.

"Your back pockets, sir."

He turned around, slid his hands in and out. "Do you want to check them yourself?" he asked, sneering.

"Your jacket," she said, her mouth set, her eyes not even looking at me.

Jay pulled out the linings and a couple of wads of fluff drifted to the floor.

Patricia's cheeks flushed. "Would you take it off, please?"

"Stupid retard," Jay mumbled as he peeled off the jacket.

I shut my eyes. I saw against the back of my

eyelids a bunch of sixth graders circling Patricia and me. *"Retard, Retard," they chanted. I felt her strong hand grip mine. "Ignore them," she told me. "Just ignore them." Never let them see that it hurts.* I opened my eyes. The images and the voices disappeared.

Patricia patted down the jacket.

"My parents are going to sue you, you moron."

I just couldn't ignore him. I hated Patricia in that moment. Not because she was reacting like a brick wall to all of this, not because she'd done something dumb and humiliated the coolest boyfriend I'd ever had — my only boyfriend, in fact. But because she'd done something even waiting for forty minutes by a water fountain, and a cheese bubble on Jay's chin, could not do.

"Remove your hat, sir."

"Satisfied, idiot?" he asked as he held his empty cap in front of her.

Patricia had made me fall out of love with Jay, and I didn't think I could ever forgive her. I couldn't hold it in any longer. "Shut up, Jay. My sister's not an idiot!"

Jay's mouth dropped but I stomped off, not looking back.

I walked outside into a cold rain and watched a bus pull away from my stop. I didn't care. My stomach clenched around a hard rock of disappointment. I couldn't cry. I stared at the Ts jeans ad on the bus shelter. A terrifically thin and good-looking couple held onto each other's waists, which were bare because their T-shirts didn't quite cover their navels. The girl and guy stared out at me. They looked angry, as angry as I felt. Why are you watching us? their eyes seemed to demand. We want to kiss some more. Only their lips looked bruised and puffy, as though they'd already been kissing for hours. If you're thin, you get lots of love, lots of kisses, and live happily ever after, right?

Wrong. It was all a lie. Jay had turned into a toad without even a single pucker. I could be as thin as I wanted — there was no happily ever after. I would never buy those jeans again.

I began to run and my feet splashed puddle water all up my legs.

RETARD! STUPID! IDIOT! Those sixth graders behind my eyelids chanted at me now. They all sounded like Jay, but they were insulting me, not my sister. Finally, I slowed down and walked the long way home, pounding out those voices with every footstep.

The phone rang as I stepped into the house a couple of hours later. I scooped it up.

"You're back. How did it go?" It was Steph.

"Awful." And then I couldn't say anything else.

Stephanie listened to my breathing for a couple of seconds. "I'll be right over," she finally said when I didn't continue.

"No, Steph?"

"Yeah?"

"Can I sleep over there? I don't want to be here when Patricia gets home."

"Patricia? Um — sure. I'll meet you halfway."

I hung up the phone and then wondered why the house was so quiet. "Nan? Naaa-aan?" No answer. I walked around. It was normal for Mom to host Saturday open houses, but Nan was like the television, always there. I flicked it on so the house wouldn't be so quiet as I packed my bag.

Before I left, I wrote a note for the fridge. As I pulled off a magnet to stick my note up in clear view I noticed Mom's scribbled message to me.

Lauren,

We're at emergency. Will call you later. Mom.

Nan must be sick! Had she been taking those gold injections? I'd been so wrapped up in my dieting and working out, I wasn't sure. *You could end up in a wheelchair*, Mom had told Nan. Could she die? When was the last time I'd sat down to watch The Shopping Network with her? I chewed at my baby fingernail.

I'll call Mom's office and have her paged, I thought. But as I reached for the phone I spotted the little black box — her pager — sitting on the kitchen counter. So much for that.

Should I just go to the hospital? I wondered. No, by now Stephanie would be waiting, I had to meet her. Besides, maybe Nan was all through at Emergency and in the car on her way home. I turned off the TV, slung my backpack over one shoulder and hoisted up my duffle bag. When I found myself power walking, I slowed down. Was there any point? All that work to become a knockout for a guy who looked like a stud muffin but acted like a scum bucket. Just how good, exactly, did slim feel?

"Mom took Nan to Emergency," I told Steph the moment I saw her. Her hair was streaming down her face, she had waited in the rain so long for me.

"Really? Well, don't worry. Mom takes Grandpa to Emergency whenever she can't get an appointment with his regular doctor."

I looked down at my feet.

"C'mon, Nan's probably fine." Steph threw her arm around my shoulders. "So, what's this about avoiding Patricia?" She watched my face for a second. "Lauren?" she said gently.

Finally, I told her what had happened back at the Economart.

"Did he really steal something?" Stephanie asked.

"Well, no. I mean, she made him do everything but undress. And who knows, maybe she did that after I left." We walked along together toward her house.

Stephanie frowned. "Patricia's not like that though, is she? I mean, before she does something she has to be sure. Do you think she'd accuse Jay, especially if he was walking with you, unless she was positive?"

I shrugged my shoulders. "Aw, I don't know with her sometimes. She's so weird about cop stuff, she's like another person when it comes to her job."

"Maybe she saw him steal something, only he hid it somewhere." Stephanie stopped under the overhang of the video store. "Do you want to rent a game?"

"Let me check if I have enough money." I unlatched the top of my pack and loosened the drawstring. A bag of batteries lay on top. "Here hold these for a second, I forgot to give them back to Jay." As I pulled out the bag to hand them to Stephanie, I noticed it —

The new Dozers CD.

Stephanie bit at her lip and raised her eyebrows.

"Aw, what did I ever see in that guy, Steph? And he actually threatened to sue Patricia." I shook my head. Now I didn't hate Patricia any more. I hated myself. I slumped against the brick wall, held my head in my hand and stared into the open bag.

"What are you going to do?" Stephanie asked.

"I'll have to give it to Patricia. Jay will get into big trouble."

"Mmmm." Steph nodded. "This is bigger than just renting a video."

"Yeah, you know what I'd really like to do?"

"No, what?"

"Make fudge."

"Are you sure? What about your little food diary there? Didn't you use up all your thingamajigs?"

"I'm sure. It's something I really have to do."

First we picked up "Frankenbeast" again from the video store, then we made a dash next door for chocolate and nuts for the big cure. We ran the last couple of blocks to Stephanie's house and turned onto the walkway.

By the time we stepped into her house, we were both soggy and shivering. "I'll get us some towels. Come on up to my bedroom," Stephanie suggested.

She flicked on every light along the way and turned on her stereo full blast. I plunked down on her beanbag chair and she threw me her favourite beach towel, the cow one. I covered my head with it.

"C'mon, dry yourself. I gave you Lucy."

"I'm honoured." I rubbed my hair with the towel.

"You want me to blow dry your hair? We can give each other make-overs."

"Fudge first," I growled. "Honestly, Steph, I'm sorry."

"About what."

"About, you know, going ballistic over this weight-losing thing. I wasted so much time going to Weight Whippers and Select Women, counting fats . . . "

"I spend an awful lot of time on the basketball court." Stephanie grinned. "But you know, basketball's over now. Why don't I come with you to the gym?"

"Because it's boring."

"Does it have a pool?"

I tossed Lucy from my head. "Yeah, yeah it does. And you know, I've never swum in it yet."

"So then don't be sorry about anything. You look great. And some of that stuff you learned at Weight Whippers was interesting. I'm drinking more water lately." She pointed to her nose. "Notice, no zits. I think it's the water. Maybe tomorrow you can take me swimming at your gym."

"Maybe I can win a water bottle or T-shirt."

"Hey, anything's possible. Let's go make fudge."

I might have the worst taste in guys, but I did have the greatest taste in best friends.

Just in case Patricia was home already I called. I wanted her to know she'd been right all along, and I wanted to get it over with as soon as possible. I also thought she'd give me good news about Nan. No answer.

After we finished boiling up the sugar and chocolate and setting it in the fridge to harden, and licking all the spoons and bowls, I tried again. Still no answer.

"Do you really think Nan's all right?" I asked Stephanie as I hung up the receiver.

"Oh sure. It just takes hours to get looked at. What time's Patricia supposed to be home?"

I glanced at my watch. "Around now. Sometimes she shoots pool with the other security guards, though."

"So just forget about everything for now. There's nothing you can do anyway. Here, have a glass of water."

We both downed a couple of glasses, rinsing the chocolate sweetness from our mouths. Then I called home again. *Ring, ring, ring, ring.* It was the loneliest sound.

We played "Frankenbeast" for a couple of hours, but between each round I tried phoning home. Still no luck.

Then Steph's mom came home from shopping with her dad. As we helped her unload the groceries, the phone rang.

"Hello. Why yes, she's here. Uh huh . . . uh huh . . . Ohhhh! Is she all right? Uh huh . . . uh huh. Yes, I'll drive her right over."

I cringed as I listened. Something had to be really wrong with Nan.

"Get your coat, Lauren. I'm going to drive you to your mom. She's waiting for you at St. Jo's."

"Is everything all right?"

"There's nothing for you to worry about. Your mom will explain what's happened when you see her."

That meant it had to be even more serious than I thought. I mean, if Nan had to stay for tests, she would have just said that, wouldn't she?

Stephanie gave me a hug.

I grabbed my backpack, and Stephanie and I climbed into Mrs. Kowalski's van. She drove like a turtle, and by the time we got to St. Jo's I'd chewed down my second baby fingernail and started on my thumb.

Mom rushed up to us when she saw us and threw her arms around me. "Patricia's going to be fine."

"Patricia?"

"Yes, Nan's with her right now." Mom grabbed my elbow and hustled me through the foyer of the hospital.

"Mom, Patricia?" I stopped her.

"Mrs. Kowalski didn't tell you anything?"

"No."

"Patricia was involved in . . . an altercation. She was asked to disperse some inebriated — "

"Mom, stop trying to increase my word power!"

"Patricia threw a drunk out of the mall. Only he doubled back after and jumped her when she wasn't looking." Mom grabbed my elbow again and led me toward the elevator. "Come on. She specifically wants to see you."

"How bad is she?"

Mom pushed the UP button and then turned to face me. "It only looks bad, honey."

It was the "honey" that got to me. "Mom!"

Mom sniffed and wiped around her eyes with her thumb. "She needed ten stitches above the eye and her face is bruised. They're keeping her overnight for observation."

We stepped into a crowded elevator, and as it lifted up, I felt my stomach drop, bowling-ball hard.

Two floors up, we stepped out. "They just brought her up from Emergency when I called," Mom explained. "Do I look okay? We don't want her to think we're upset." She sniffed again.

I swallowed hard and nodded.

Arm in arm, we walked down the longest hall in the world, turning into a room near the end.

"Patricia!" In a flash I took in her swollen grape-coloured face and the red slash above her brow. Then I just ran to her and held her tight so that nothing bad would ever happen to her again.

"Hey, you're hurting me, Lauren."

"Oh, sorry." I let her go and pulled away. Then I suddenly remembered. "Patricia, I found the stupid Dozers CD in my backpack. You were right, Jay did steal something."

"I knew that. It was the next place I would have looked."

"What?"

"Well, Jasmine — the shopper on duty — saw him take it. We just didn't know where he'd stashed it." Patricia smiled, making her face look even more swollen.

"You knew all along." I shook my head. "So why didn't I know?"

Patricia shrugged her shoulders, beaming now. "Hey, it's my job."

"Well, maybe now that boss of yours will give you that raise," Nan piped in.

"Nan . . . Hi, how are you?" I turned to notice her sitting in an armchair. And then I had rush over and hug her too.

"Well, this is awfully nice," Nan said, hugging me back.

"I thought *you* were the one who was sick."

"Nope. Even my fingers are good today." Nan stretched her hands in front of her.

I sat back on Patricia's bed, quivery with relief.

"Ow!" Patricia said.

"Sit on the chair," Mom told me. "Or the nurse will have your head."

I moved myself over to the other armchair, but as I did I saw someone being wheeled down the hallway. Someone whose bony arms stuck out from hospital-gown sleeves, someone whose neck sinews showed tense against her skin. She seemed like a stranger, but those huge bubble eyes staring vacantly made her also seem oddly familiar.

"Andrea?" I called.

Chapter 16

"Mom, Mom! I think that was Andrea they just wheeled by." I stood up and rushed to the door, glancing around the corner. The nurse pushing the wheelchair turned into a room three doors down. "Nah, it couldn't have been," I said, stepping back into the room, but then some nagging doubt made me check with Mom. "Could it?"

She twisted her mouth and looked down at her fingers.

"Oh my gosh. It *was* Andrea! In a wheelchair!"

She nodded. "They admitted her last night. Brenda didn't know what else she could do, Lauren."

"She could have made Andrea eat. She should have talked to her. She should have made her eat," I repeated as I paced by the door.

"It's not that simple, honey." Mom sighed heavily. "You have to know by now that Andrea's sick. She's anorexic."

"I can't believe it. Andrea's smart, Mom, A-plus, in control. This can't happen to her!"

Mom lifted her shoulders and let them drop. No

answer. She just sat there, shaking her head.

"I have to go see her. Patricia, I'll be back in a couple of minutes."

"Lauren, you can't — "

I marched out of the room, not listening for the end of Mom's sentence. Straight down the hall to Andrea's. I tapped gently on the opened door and peered around it.

Andrea sat in the bed, her arms folded across her chest, the sheets neatly tucked around her waist. She was dressed in a blue hospital gown. Her face, shadowed by the dark hollows beneath her cheekbones, was softened by a pale fuzz. I'd never noticed that before. Otherwise she looked grey and sullen, her unsmiling lips puffy or maybe pouty. She reminded me of someone but I couldn't put my finger on who.

"Andrea?"

She didn't answer but I stepped in anyway. The room was hospital blue, to match her gown, and the furniture your basic industrial grunge. A couple of empty armchairs sat beneath the window. A table, empty except for a curved metal basin and a plastic water jug and cup, sat next to her bed. There were no flowers or cards anywhere. Even the television screen mounted near the ceiling was a blank dark grey. Andrea sat there all alone.

The bed tray covered her lap and a dish with a muffin sat on it. Andrea didn't look my way. Instead she faced the window, staring at a gravel roof.

"Andrea . . . You all right?"

She turned sharply. I'd startled her.

"Sorry. I just saw you in a wheelchair. I mean, can't you walk?"

"Lauren." Andrea smiled. "I'm glad you're here. Sit down quick. Over here so the nurses can't see you from the hall."

I did as she told me.

"Perfect. Are you hungry?" She lifted her plate and held it toward me. "Here, have a muffin."

"Uh, no I'm not, really. Thanks anyway."

"Aw c'mon, it's just a muffin." She gestured with her chin to the plate still outstretched toward me. "If it's gone, they'll leave me alone. I just want to go home, Lauren. Why can't they let me go home?"

I ignored the muffin. But what I couldn't ignore any more was what was happening to Andrea. "Andrea, why was that nurse wheeling you around?"

"They took me to the bathroom." She snarled the last part. "They don't trust me to go by myself."

"I bet you're supposed to eat this thing." I watched as Andrea's face twisted for a split second. Anger, hatred, suspicion, and then it all melted into a smile, her perfect polite Andrea smile.

"Yes, but this is a carrot muffin. I hate carrots."

"You hate *carrots?*" I looked into her eyes. Doll blue, pleading and afraid. Fat or thin, she was still the same old Andrea. "You've been living on carrots for the past three months."

"Exactly. That's why." She glanced toward the door and back at me. "Could you do it for me, please? Because you're my best friend?" She grabbed my arm and I looked down at her hand. It was clawlike, with all the bones and veins standing out clearly. Her arm was just as bad, long, pitifully thin and fuzzy like her face.

Why hadn't I noticed earlier? Because she was always wearing those baggy shirts and sweaters? Because I couldn't believe it? I inhaled deeply, wishing somehow I could say yes, I'll eat your muffin for you. It would be so easy and I wanted so badly to help her. Only I knew I couldn't. As I exhaled, I couldn't find the strength to say no. Instead, I just shook my head quickly.

"You're just like all the others." Andrea dropped the plate on the floor. Crash! The plate shattered. The muffin rolled away like a broken doll's head. "I'd rather be dead than fat again." She turned away from me.

I'd rather be dead — I couldn't believe Andrea would say that.

At that moment a nurse walked in. "What's this, then? You promised you'd eat the muffin. Andrea?"

With her arms across her chest, Andrea stared out at the gravel again, not answering.

"Are you a friend?" The nurse turned to me now.

"Uh, um . . . "

Andrea sniffed angrily. I almost expected her to deny it since I hadn't eaten her muffin.

"Yes," I finally finished.

"That's nice," the nurse said, smiling. "Only you're really not supposed to be in here. Family only. Unless of course, Andrea can eat better with company. Andrea, should I bring you something else?"

Andrea sat stiffly, biting at her lip.

"We'll have to tube feed you then."

Andrea's shoulders shook and she wiped at her face.

A *tube?* Where would they put it? "Please could you get Andrea a different muffin, maybe blueberry?" I suggested.

"It's up to Andrea."

"C'mon, Andrea," I urged. "You can do it."

"No," Andrea said quietly. "I can't."

Inside of me, the hard rock smashed into bits. "Andrea, look at your arms! They're twigs."

Instead Andrea looked back toward that gravel roof.

"Don't turn away, Andrea! I'm not like the others. Andrea, you have to start eating now."

She looked past me to the nurse. "Give me the tube," she said quietly.

How could she just lie there and not even try? How could she want a tube? I wanted to shake Andrea so badly that I had to leave.

I dashed out of that lonely room, down the hall, back to the warm friendly one where Patricia sat, now watching "Wheel of Fortune" with Nan and Mom. I slumped down on the edge of the bed and immediately Mom's hand touched my shoulder. I looked over at Nan and tried to smile when she winked at me. But I felt so mad at Andrea, I ended up squeezing back tears instead.

"That's all right, Lauren," Nan told me. "You sit there and help us now. Patricia just lost the car. Maybe you can try for the dream vacation."

"You say she *wanted* the tube?" Stephanie floated on her back in the pool. We were all by ourselves on the top floor of the Select Women building.

"Yes, she wouldn't even try to eat." I punched at the water in a splashy dog-paddle.

"That's so weird. But then when Andrea makes up her mind, you know how she is."

"Yeah, I guess." I grabbed hold of an edge of the pool and kicked as hard as I could for a while. The water bubbled up as angry as I felt. "I tried to be her friend. I *tried*, Stephanie."

"C'mon. You are her friend." Stephanie floated to the edge and grabbed on too. "Just because you don't like her as much as say . . .

me," Stephanie smiled, "doesn't mean it's your fault she's sick."

"But I went along with all the dieting too. I gave that speech. I made those jokes." I kicked again furiously. "I can't enter the public speaking competition now."

Stephanie waited till I stopped. "You sure?"

"Oh, yeah, I'm going to get everyone to laugh at Jon Minnoch again just because he was fat. I'm going to say how easy it is to diet and that anyone with a bit of willpower can do it."

"But you've been looking forward to it since forever. Since grade one!" Steph chewed her lip awhile. "Why don't you change the speech then, Lauren?"

"I don't know . . . What I can say?"

"Aw, you'll come up with something. Something really good too."

I swam across the pool, worrying about Andrea, wondering how I had gone so far overboard. Writing down everything I ate, weighing it, weighing myself, exercising frantically — it all seemed so stupid now. And yet staying fat, growing into some kind of piano person that needed to be hauled into her grave with a crane — that seemed wrong too.

Stephanie floated by on her back again. "How's Patricia doing, anyway?"

"Great. Her boss called this morning after we brought her home from the hospital. He gave her the week off and a raise, and he agreed she could take her holidays in June so we can all visit Dad."

"Great! Did Patricia tell her boss about the CD?" Stephanie flipped over and paddled toward me.

"No. I'm going to do that. But first I need to talk to Jay." I kicked madly again.

Stephanie kicked along with me. When the bubbles subsided she turned to me. "You know, this is the life. Our own private pool. I'd join Select Women just for this."

I shrugged my shoulders, then dove to the bottom and did a handstand. "Did you count how long I held it?" I asked her when I came back up.

"At least ten Saskatchewans. You count for me now." Stephanie dove and I watched her feet point toward the ceiling.

"Eleven," I told her when she surfaced. "You're right. This is the life. And I never came here once with Andrea."

"Ts jeans, Lauren?" Kim asked as we stood in line at the cafeteria the next day.

"They were on sale," I explained. I'd considered taking them back because of that bus shelter ad, but my receipt had been stamped FINAL SALE. I motioned to Mrs. Fatawa for a plate of lasagna.

Kim tilted her head to one side, assessing the effect of the jeans on my body. "When your hips slim down some more, the jeans'll look even better." She reached across me for her salad.

I felt my face flush hot.

"You know, my cousin in Alberta lost a lot of weight on this really great diet. She ate nothing but liverwurst and ice cream for two months." Kim set her salad down on her tray, not noticing my face at all.

"Liverwurst and ice cream? I thought it was rice cakes."

"Rice cakes? No, that was a diet Jay heard about on the Web." Kim shrugged her shoulders and tilted her head. Another pose for some invisible camera. "Heard you went out with him." Now she raised her eyebrows into arrows that she aimed my way. We slid our trays along. "Told you he'd think you were cute if you lost weight."

Inside my head, a buzzer sounded. *Ehhhhhh!* Wrong. That wasn't what Kim had told me before. "Noooo," I told Kim. I paid the cashier and slammed a set of cutlery onto my tray.

"What do you mean, no? He went out with you, didn't he?" Kim smiled.

"You told me he thought I was cute the way I was, but that I would be a knockout if I lost weight."

"Oh. Is that what I said?" Kim giggled. "Well, so what? It made you lose the weight, didn't it? Of course he's going to like you better if you look better."

It was funny just how ugly Kim looked to me right then. The voice in my head was screaming now. "You made it all up!" I snapped. "What did he really say when you asked him if he liked me?"

Kim pursed her lips and glared back at me. "You honestly want to know?"

"Yes."

"He said you were cute, but I was way cuter." Kim tossed her hair back over her shoulder. "So now you know." Her eyes gloated for a moment. Then she flounced away.

With everything still boiling hot inside me, I figured now was a good time to face Jay. Tray in hand, I followed Kim to the boys' table. "Could I speak to you a minute, Jay? Alone?" I asked.

"I'm busy right now," he said as he pulled out a chair for Kim.

"All right then. I'll talk to you right here." I banged down my tray on his table and then reached into my backpack. "These are your batteries. You forgot them."

"Yeah, thanks. I did." He shifted around in his chair.

"But this here, this isn't yours." I pulled out the Dozers CD and held it up for him to see. "You stole it from Economart."

Jay shrugged his shoulders.

"I'm returning it to the store manager and explaining how you stashed it in my backpack. That is . . . unless you want to take it back yourself."

Carlos and Matt jerked forward in their chairs.

"Aw man, she can't do that, Jay."

"Don't worry about it." White spots appeared on Jay's cheeks. "He's never going to believe her anyway. It was in *her* bag!"

"I take that as a no. Fine, I'll go by myself." I tossed the CD next to my lasagna, picked up the tray again and headed back to eat with Stephanie.

"He wouldn't return it, would he?" Stephanie said as I sat down.

"No. And you know what makes me maddest about the whole thing?" I grabbed hold of my fork and knife and slashed across my lasagna.

"Well, sticking the CD in your bag? That would have ticked me off."

"Isn't that the lowest? But no, that wasn't it. It was the way he called Patricia all kinds of names. Stupid, Idiot . . . I don't know, he just got me so mad." I slashed at the lasagna again. "And I thought to myself, if only Patricia had made a dumb mistake, then I could still like Jay. But I knew that I couldn't. Because of the names."

Stephanie nodded. "I'll go with you, Lauren."

"Do you mean it?"

"Sure," she said, sipping from her new Select Women water bottle. "We can do it on the way to the pool tomorrow. Maybe we can win a T-shirt."

It wasn't as rough as I expected. At the Customer Service Desk I asked for Jock, Patricia's boss, and when I told him who I was he smiled and insisted on buying Steph and me Cokes.

I swallowed hard before I handed him the CD. "Here."

He stared at it.

"I'm really sorry. A friend of mine stole it and hid it in my bag. Honestly, I had no idea."

Jock shook the disc in the air. "Ah yes, he's the shoplifter Jasmine picked out. Thank you."

"Am I going to have to testify against him?" I asked, hoping the answer would be no.

"Would you be willing to?" He looked me straight in the eye.

I took a deep breath. "Yes, sir."

"Well, that's good." He downed the rest of his coffee. "But we ordinarily can't press charges unless we catch the person with the goods. Don't worry, though, we'll get him next time." He stood up and patted me on the shoulder. "It was good of you to stop by and see me. Say hello to Patricia for me."

And that was it.

We won the Select Women tote bag after our swim. As we headed home I stopped near the bus shelter and pointed to the ad. "That's it! That's who Andrea reminds me of."

"What are you talking about?"

"When I visited her in the hospital, there was

something about her face. She looked angry like they do. Her cheekbones stick out just like theirs."

"They do kind of look mad at the world, don't they?"

"You don't think Ts would hire anorexic models, do you?"

Stephanie shrugged her shoulders. "Who knows? But if it would sell jeans, maybe they would."

Chapter 17

"Brenda asked me if you'd visit Andrea this afternoon," Mom said. "She turns fourteen today."

"Oh gees, it's her birthday. But Mom, she hates me now."

Mom sighed. "She's sick, Lauren, you know that. She's saying things she doesn't mean, she's angry at everyone."

"She wasn't always angry like that," I said, remembering. "You know how she is with Neil and Noah." I pictured Andrea sitting in that blue hospital gown. "Mom, Andrea looks so different. Not just that she's thin. Her face and arms are all fuzzy."

Mom shook her head. "Yes, that's part of her illness. Anorexics sometimes get that."

I felt vaguely sick now. "Does she really have a tube?"

Mom frowned and nodded.

"Where?"

"They put it in her nose."

"I don't think I can face her."

"I understand." Mom said it in a low discouraged voice.

I wished she didn't feel that way, but she hadn't been in that room with Andrea. She didn't know how hard it was to be her friend at the best of times. Besides, I'd already made plans for my day. I needed to go to my Weight Whippers meeting because despite how good that fudge tasted, I decided I still wanted to keep those ten extra pounds off. And then after, Steph and I were going to swim at the Select Women pool. Stephanie wanted to join, and we thought if no one was in the pool, we might film a low-budget Barbie/Jaws movie. Mom had become pretty relaxed about me using her camcorder since we'd done the Eggs Men. I really didn't have time to see Andrea.

Even if she didn't have that tube.

At the Weight Whippers meeting I raised my hand and told about my difficult moment with a tray of chocolate fudge. "At the time, it tasted way better than slim felt," I told them.

All the women laughed except for Kate Luzinsky. She frowned for a moment and then suggested if we couldn't just take one taste, or one slice of a dessert, then it might be a trigger food. "If you can't resist your trigger food, then you're better off leaving it alone entirely. Don't buy any, don't even look at any."

That seemed pretty extreme to me, but since Steph and I don't usually keep vats of fudge lying around anyway, it didn't matter.

I weighed the same as last week so Kate told me not to worry about my little setback. "You're still on track. Just eat sensibly."

After the meeting broke up I strolled to the mall, where I'd agreed to meet Steph under the palm tree at the famous fountain of love.

She didn't get there right away, and as I was waiting I noticed a new stand in the middle of the aisle nearby. There were lifelike statues of animals sitting on the table. One of them, a wild-eyed black stallion, reared up on his hind legs, kicking. "Andrea would like that," I told Stephanie when she joined me.

"It's beautiful," Stephanie agreed.

"Andrea turns fourteen today."

Stephanie picked up the statue. "Eighteen ninety-five," she read from the price sticker. "Do you have enough?"

"No, I guess not. Besides I can't face her, not when she hates me the way she does." I looked down at my shoes for a moment. "And she's still got the tube in her nose."

Stephanie put the stallion down. "My grandfather had that when he went in for his heart. The first time I saw it I thought I'd barf. But you know, I got used it after a few minutes."

I looked back up at the stallion, knowing it was perfect for Andrea. But I only had eight dollars on me. "Do you have any money, Steph?"

"A couple of dollars."

"Well, I guess that's my answer then. I won't visit Andrea." I felt relieved as we left the display and crossed the street to the gym.

Stephanie handed in her membership application and I grabbed for the pool key.

But later as I stood beside the pool, my zoom lens fixed on Barbie bobbing in the aqua water, with the little grey rubber shark approaching her, my mind kept drifting to Andrea, all by herself on her birthday, not even wanting to eat cake.

"Maybe we could find a smaller stallion that costs less," I finally said to Steph.

"I'm sure we can," she agreed. "The two dollars are yours too. You don't have to pay me back."

We changed back into street clothes, but as we headed for the exit Cherry stopped us. "Hey, your friend joined, Lauren. Don't forget to pick your bonus balloon."

I chose a pink one and we covered our ears as Cherry popped it.

"Whoo hooo! Twenty-five dollars!" Cherry jumped into the air like a cheerleader at halftime.

She pumped at my hand and then went to the back office, returning with a couple of tens and a five. "Here you go! Thanks for joining, Stephanie."

"Welcome." Stephanie gave her a two-fingered wave and we left.

"Now we can buy the stallion we liked."

"Pretty neat, huh?" Stephanie smiled.

The man at the display giftwrapped the stallion for me in satiny plum-coloured paper. Then he carefully tied a blue ribbon around it and curled the ends with a scissor blade until the bow turned into a little explosion of ringlets.

Stephanie helped me make a card for Andrea on one of those Express Yourself computers. We chose a newspaper card where we had to write the headline. "Extra! Extra! Read All About It. Andrea Partington Leaps Over Another Hurdle." And in the first line, we keyed in, "Andrea Reached the Big 1-4 Today." Inside I just typed Happy Birthday. "Should I sign your name, Stephanie?"

"No, this is from you. I'm going to pick her up something in the grocery store. You wait for the card, I'll be back in a sec."

"Okay." I filled in the back of the card: "A Best Friend Production," and then pressed PRINT. Two minutes later the card rolled out. I folded it and tucked it in one of the cream-coloured envelopes.

Stephanie returned with a small grocery bag in her hand. "Can you lend me some money for the bus?" she asked.

"Sure." We headed for the shelter and I stared at the Ts Jeans poster again as we waited.

"The bus!" Stephanie shook me. "It's here. Let's go!"

It wasn't a long ride to St. Jo's, but as the bus rolled in front of the hospital I suddenly lost my nerve again. "I can't do it, Steph. I just can't."

"C'mon. Just don't look at the tube. You'll be fine."

A moment later we climbed down the steps of the bus and walked up to the hospital's front entrance. "But it's not the look of the tube," I told Stephanie. "It's the fact that she chose it over eating, that I can't take."

"I know." Stephanie frowned. "What do you want to do?"

I stared at the beautifully wrapped stallion, thinking it might really cheer Andrea up. "Maybe we can just drop off the present and card at the nursing station."

"Yeah, that would work. And if you change your mind . . . "

"I can't."

"Well, all right." We headed to the elevator and I pressed the floor button. The door opened in seconds, and Stephanie and I walked slower and slower toward the station.

"Mom says it's just because she's sick and she doesn't mean it, but if you'd seen how angry Andrea was at me, Steph . . . She wouldn't even look at me." We passed the nursing station now and stepped closer and closer to Andrea's room. "I don't know what to say to her."

"And it's not like you're her best friend or anything, is it?" Stephanie asked. She held out the grocery bag toward me. "Here," she said softly. "Tell her it's from her lunch-table partner. I'll wait for you downstairs."

"Don't . . . " Go, I wanted to say. But Stephanie was already down the hall. I took a breath and tapped on the door.

"Come in," a tired voice said.

This time Andrea faced me right away. Otherwise I wouldn't have seen the tube immediately. Only slightly bigger than the nose jewellery some of Patricia's friends wear, the small yellow tube led from her left nostril across her cheek, where a piece of surgical tape held it in place, down to dangle beneath her chin. Instead of eating, she chose this. How *could* she? I guess I only thought she had everything under control. Now finally I realized how sick Andrea had to be. "Hi, happy birthday."

"Thank you." Andrea didn't invite me to sit down or anything, but I pulled up an armchair from beneath the window anyway. A bouquet of bright flowers with a teddy bear holding onto a heart sat next to her metal basin now. Cards stood around it.

"Did you get new pyjamas?" I asked. Instead of a hospital gown, she wore a bright red flannel jacket.

Andrea nodded. "For my birthday."

"They're nice."

She nodded again.

"Here, I bought you something." I placed the package in front of her and she stared at it for a long time. "Well go on, open it."

Andrea touched the bow gently with her fingers. "You didn't have to."

"Well, I just saw — um — something that reminded me so much of you, that I needed to buy it. Do you want me to help you?"

"No. I can do it." Andrea looked toward the gravel roof for a moment. Finally she turned back and pulled off the ribbon. She carefully picked off every piece of tape till I thought I would go crazy waiting. She folded up the wrapping paper neatly and placed the ribbon on top.

"Would you pul-ease open it!"

Andrea smiled a little as she lifted the flap. "An Arabian," she sighed. Then she closed her eyes.

"What's the matter. Don't you like it?"

She opened her eyes again. "I love him. He's perfect." She gently lifted the stallion from the box and sat there holding it, not saying anything else.

"Well, like I said, he reminded me of you." The day you decided to diet, I thought, but didn't say it.

"*I'm* not perfect," Andrea whispered. Her eyes shone, huge and blue, doll-like.

Don't cry, Andrea, don't cry. "Aw well, you know, who is?" I said, but now a tear slid down my cheek. "Here, this is from Steph." I plunked down the grocery bag. "She said to tell you it's from your lunch buddy."

Andrea first pulled out a tiny box of birthday candles, then a package of matches and finally two cellophane-wrapped cupcakes, the chocolate kind with the white squiggles.

I wiped the tear from my face. "Let's pull that tray thing around here so we can do this right." I set it up, placed the stallion to one side, then put the cupcakes, complete with candles, in the middle. Try fitting fourteen candles on two little cupcakes. It wasn't easy. And then one for good luck. I lit them, one by one.

"Happy birthday, dear Andrea, happy birthday to you," I sang softly. "Make a wish."

The soft glow of the candles reflected off her face, making it look less shadowed. Happy, almost. Her cheeks puffed out for a second as she blew all the tiny flames out. "I just want to go home," she sighed when the glow disappeared.

"C'mon, you can't tell what your wish is. It won't come true." I tried to say the words lightly but didn't quite carry it off, when I noticed Andrea's eyes filling. "Are you going to eat your cupcakes?" I whispered. Of course that was my wish.

She shook her head. "I had a tiny piece of birthday cake with Mom and the twins." She cupped her hands near her blanket-covered waist. "And my stomach's still bulging out. It's awful."

A large hard silence seemed to stick in my throat. "Sooo . . . . " I started, knowing I needed to talk now while I still could. "Steph joined Select Women. We tried the pool and there's never anyone in it because it's so far from the actual gym. When you get out of here, you can come swim with us. And when you get back to school, we're working on descriptive stories — no more speeches. You'll like that."

She shook her head.

"What, don't you like swimming?" There was that look in Andrea's eyes again, pleading. "You don't like description? I know I'd rather write action or dialogue but . . . "

"I'm not coming back to school," Andrea said.

"But what about your A average?"

"I'm taking special tutorials in here. There's only three weeks left anyway. And . . . when they let me go," her eyes shone now, her voice became strong, "I might be moving in with my dad."

"But he lives in Vancouver, doesn't he?"

She nodded and continued. "Mom's thinking that maybe I need a change . . . that with her working weekends and evenings, plus with the twins around, she doesn't have enough time to spend with me." Andrea frowned for a moment and then grumbled, "The doctor told her about a special eating disorder treatment centre in Victoria. You know I don't need it, but . . . but Mom . . . well . . . "

"Oh Andrea," I said softly.

"Dad's slim now too. He runs every day, and he says he's planning to enter the Boston Marathon."

Why should that matter? I wondered. And then the answer hit me like a piano case in the gut: Because Andrea's still not cured. "Well, maybe it's for the best then," I said. Maybe she did need that treatment centre.

"Nothing's really been decided," she went on. "It's all up to me. But Dad wants me. I spoke to him today. He's really excited." She paused and then spoke louder, brightening with her flashbulb smile. "He says I can have my own horse. A real horse of my own, Lauren."

"Too bad Vancouver is so far away."

Andrea's smile faded and her voice broke. Her eyes filled but they didn't spill over. "I'd miss Noah and Neil so much."

Was it really up to her? Could she still get her wish to just go home? I couldn't take it any more. My throat hurt and a rock ached somewhere in my chest as I leaned over and hugged Andrea, feeling every bone through her flannel pyjama top. Andrea didn't cry, but I couldn't stop the tears sliding down my cheeks.

Andrea was still in the hospital two weeks later as I walked up the stage steps to give my presentation. When I took my place at the podium in the centre of the stage and adjusted the mike for my height, I glanced at rows of full seats. Then I grasped both sides of the podium and smiled at the sea of faces. I took my extra moment to make eye contact, but it stretched into two and then three as I noticed all the different shapes of people sitting in front of me. One judge looked pointy and bullet-headed, another flowed over her chair. Round and square faces, curved and angular. The bullet-headed judge coughed and I realized I had better start my speech. I took a deep cleansing breath, in through the nose, out through the mouth.

"Jon Brower Minnoch, the heaviest human in medical history, weighed almost fourteen hundred pounds." I paused to allow time for the tittering from the kids at the back. "When he sat around the house, he *really* sat around the house." Now there were louder snickers. "It was rumoured that he was baptised at Marineland." As I paused the second time, kids laughed openly. Even the overflowing judge chuckled.

I didn't laugh. I stared down at the podium and in my mind heard Matt and Carlos whinnying at Andrea when she gave her horse talk.

"When Minnoch suffered from heart and respiratory problems, a dozen firemen carried him by special stretcher to a ferry, which took him to the hospital. They lashed two beds together, and it took thirteen people just to turn him over." Again kids tittered, this time maybe a little nervously when they realized I wasn't smiling. A teacher guffawed and then looked uncomfortable as a few people turned around to stare at him.

I took in a deep breath and tried to smile. "That's okay, don't worry. The whole world thinks it's all right to make fun of fat people." Another breath. "We think overweight people are lazy and sloppy, with no self-control."

For a moment I saw a flash of Andrea, wild like her stallion, vowing to become thin and vowing to be perfect. I shook my head, and bit my lips.

"I have a friend who used to be overweight. She was the neatest, most controlled person I've ever known. Well, she still is. But she couldn't take people laughing at her so she decided to diet. And she's been very successful at the losing game.

"Andrea recently told me from her hospital bed that she'd rather die than be fat."

I closed my eyes then. They were burning and I needed to concentrate hard on clearing the tears from them. Somewhere in the distance the whispering and chair shuffling called me back. Finally I swallowed the enormous rock in my throat, opened my eyes and looked up at the audience, unsmiling.

"I played the losing game too. I joined a health club and Weight Whippers. I thought when I lost some weight I'd be beautiful and then I'd find true love." I reached into my back pocket now and unfolded a magazine version of the bus shelter ad. "Like this guy and girl here wearing Ts jeans. Sure these are beautiful people. They have clear perfect skin, and terrific mouths — but look closely at their bodies. Aren't they really too thin?

"And you know, it's okay for some people to be on the skinny side too. Only, for some reason, Ts and other companies have decided that thin is in, and the rest of us torture ourselves to fit their image." I held up *The Guinness Book of Records* picture of the tribal woman with the plate distending her mouth. "Just like this woman from Surma, where they decided dishes between their lips were really beautiful." I put the book down on the podium.

"Or in China, where women used to bind their feet till they couldn't even walk, just so their feet would stay small and what someone had decided was pretty. Or in the western world, women used to wear corsets so tight, their organs would be displaced. All because someone decided women's waists should be tiny.

"My Nan told me that a hundred years ago, plumper women were considered more beautiful. Even when she was growing up, a girl my size would be considered thin. Who decides all this?

"My friend Andrea says that you can never be thin enough. And this ad," I held up the Ts jeans poster again, "seems to go along with that idea."

Sweeping my arm around me to make sure everyone got a good look at the picture this time, I said nothing, chewing the inside of my mouth instead. I shook my head and finally folded the poster up.

"Ever notice that the first part of the word *diet* is *die?* Are we all dying to be thin?" I looked around the room again. All those faces — round and square, curved and angular, black and white. For a moment I lost track of where I was in the presentation, I'd thrown in so much at the last minute.

"Jon Minnoch dieted. Do you know that he lost the most weight on record: 911 pounds in 16 months?

"Unfortunately, he also gained the most weight: 176 pounds in 7 days. This occurred after his successful weight loss.

"It's a fact that 249 out of 250 dieters cannot keep the extra pounds from coming back. When Jon Brower Minnoch died he'd gained back close to 400 pounds." I looked at all the faces again.

"I'm not saying it's always wrong to try to lose weight, although it seems close to impossible to keep it off. Only really, truthfully, looks shouldn't be everything to us, especially when we jeopardize our health to fit fashion's idea of looking good."

I stepped a little closer to the microphone. "Who decides what beautiful is?

"*We* should decide. Because plates in our mouths, tiny feet, small waists or even skinny bodies, don't guarantee us love. And we should decide against a kind of beauty that makes us fight our bodies.

"We also shouldn't laugh at anyone for their physical appearance. Or for any reason, for that matter. We should look for what's inside them. And we definitely shouldn't make it so awful for heavy people that they'd rather die than be fat." I paused, to make eye contact again.

"Do you know that the thinnest people in the world suffer from anorexia nervosa? Statistics show that five to ten percent of these people actually die from this losing game."

"Jon Brower Minnoch weighed the most, lost the most and gained the most. His whole life became a statistic for a book. And then he died." I had to take a deep breath.

"And my friend Andrea? My perfect thin friend, Andrea?" I looked up at the ceiling for a moment, but it didn't help. I felt tears slide down my face. "Andrea has anorexia nervosa. And right now, she's not doing too well."

I couldn't say anything more. My throat shut and the audience became a big wet blur. And I knew it was a rotten ending. I knew it from the shocked silence that lasted what seemed like forever as everyone waited to see if I would go on. Only there was no other ending to give.

Somebody from the back of the room let out a

sob. I heard someone else sniffling.

"Thank you," I finally said with a slight bow of my head. Slowly, like a ripple in a lake, the clapping began. The judges in the front row, then teachers and finally the students too. I nodded, smiled as I wiped around my eyes, and then marched down the steps.

Ms Smyrnios ran after me as I continued to the exit. "Wait, Lauren. Wait." She took me in her arms. It was the first time since kindergarten that a teacher had done that. "It was a wonderful speech. You've been a very good friend to Andrea."

I shook my head. "No, I don't think so."

There was a reception following the speeches, where the winners were announced. Ms Smyrnios made me go. I wasn't shocked or disappointed when I didn't win. I'd stopped too many times, gone off topic and not given them a conclusive ending.

As parents and students grabbed coffees and juice, we all milled around the food. Trays full of nanaimo bars, brownies and tarts covered one table. Plates of veggies and crackers and cheese covered the next. The bullet-headed judge took a little paper plate of squares. The overflowing one snapped into a celery stick. And me? I stood there, quietly watching.

*Sylvia would like to thank
Dr. Miriam Kaufman
of the Hospital for Sick Children
for her invaluable input.*

*Emily Lucille Urbaniak appears in cameo as a
result of her mom's generous and winning bid in
the Peel Children's Aid Auction*

Sylvia McNicoll's favourite breakfast is leftover birthday cake with lots of icing. Not surprisingly, she has quit "the losing game" herself. She is happily married, has three great children, plus a home in Burlington with a view, a basketball net and a ping-pong table.

Some of Sylvia's books include *Bringing Up Beauty*, (winner of the Silver Birch Award), *Jump Start*, *Facing the Enemy*, *More Than Money*, *The Tiger Catcher's Kid*, *Blueberries and Whipped Cream*, *The Big Race* and *Project Disaster*.

When she isn't writing, Sylvia makes frequent school visits and acts as an on-line writer-in-residence. Check out her Web site (http://~netaccess.on.ca/~mcnicoll) for more information on Sylvia's books, plus the recipe for Nan's reverse chocolate chip cookies.